THE BOYFRIEND TRAP

Mary Hooper knows more than most people what makes a good story – she's had over six hundred published in teenage and women's magazines and she's also a reader of unsolicited fiction for IPC Magazines. In addition, she's the highly regarded author of twenty full-length titles for young people, including *Lexie* and, for Walker Books, *Spook Spotting* and *Best Friends, Worst Luck*. She's married with two children.

Books by the same author

Best Friends, Worst Luck
Janey's Diary
The Revolting Bridesmaid
School Friends
Spook Spotting

THE BOYFRIEND TRAP

MARY HOOPER

WALKER BOOKS
AND SUBSIDIARIES
LONDON • BOSTON • SYDNEY

First published 1994 by Walker Books Ltd
87 Vauxhall Walk, London SE11 5HJ

This edition published 1995

2 4 6 8 10 9 7 5 3 1

Printed in England

British Library Cataloguing in Publication Data
A catalogue record for this book is
available from the British Library.

ISBN 0-7445-3679-0

CONTENTS

1

FRIDAY

"Here we are," Mum said, as the taxi pulled up outside the big house where my sister's flat was. "Bit grotty, but I daresay it's all right inside."

The house was tall and narrow and had five floors and a basement area with railings across it. A half-dead climbing plant was twined round the railings and an old newspaper and assorted sweet wrappers had been blown against them and stuck there.

"Looks good to me!" I said, scrabbling on the floor of the taxi for the four plastic bags bulging with my stock of magazines.

"I do hope Sarah's here to let you in," Mum said worriedly. "She promised to come back in her lunch hour."

She paid off the taxi driver, then turned and tried to peer through the windows of the house. "Can't see a thing; I don't suppose they've ever washed those windows. And look at their dreadful old curtains! I've given better to jumble sales."

I looked and couldn't see anything wrong with anything. Mum, being a bit of a power woman, was used to staying in decent places when she went away, but I wasn't half so fussy. It was a funny, dirty old house but it was in London, where everything was supposed to be happening. London was exactly where I wanted to be.

Standing on the grey pavement with my magazines all round me, I felt a beam spreading across my face. For the first five weeks of the school holidays life had been grossly boring – but now I was here it was going to be *great*. I'd be shopping and discoing and partying and gossiping and meeting all Sarah's boyfriends and sitting up all night drinking coffee. I knew *exactly* what it was going to be like because there was a serial called *Girls Upstairs* in one of my magazines. It was about three girls and the goings-on in their love lives and it was set in a London flat just like this one.

Mum and I walked up the five crumbling steps to the front door and surveyed the range of bells and name cards. They were mostly changed and scribbled on – and even those that weren't could hardly be read because they were so faded.

"Now, which floor did she say?" Mum asked, peering at the pieces of cardboard.

"It doesn't matter if she isn't here," I said. "I'll settle in on my own. I'll have a good look round and see what I can..."

Mum put down my case with a thud. "Terri," she said. "Let's get this clear. You are not to interfere in any aspect of Sarah's life."

"I'm not going to interfere," I said indignantly. "I'm just going to be helpful. I would have thought you'd have been pleased to have a daughter who was so interested in helping other people." I pressed all the bells one by one. "Anyway, has Sarah got a boyfriend?"

"I really don't know," Mum muttered in a distracted voice, scanning the upper windows. "I don't think there's anyone special, at any rate."

"Why d'you think that is?" I asked earnestly. "Is she doing something wrong, not attracting the right sort of man...?"

"For goodness' *sake!*" Mum looked at me hard. "This is due to all those teenage comics you read, I know it is. They've given you silly ideas."

"They're called *magazines*."

"Full of tripy love stories which give a false impression of what life's really about. Not everyone goes along desperate to find a partner, you know."

I smiled at her pityingly; I couldn't expect

her to understand about true love any more –
not with all the aggro she'd had divorcing Dad.

"I mean, there was all that fuss at school
when you sent a Valentine card to Miss Rob-
bins from the caretaker."

"She was lonely…"

"And what about that lollipop man you
brought home for me that time? Eighty if he
was a day!"

"He was fifty-five!"

I think Mum was about to come out with
something else when the front door opened
and Sarah stood there waving her arms and
looking agitated.

"Stop ringing all the bells!" she shrieked.
"It's a good job everyone's at work or you'd be
in trouble." She took a breath. "You were supposed to be here an hour ago! The Sale starts
tomorrow and I haven't put the Derbyshire
out yet!"

"I know, darling," Mum said soothingly,
offering her cheek for a kiss and not getting
one. "We were right on schedule and then Terri
helped me collate some papers for the conference and before I knew it they'd all got butter
on them."

"And a bit of jam," I added.

"So I had to rush down to the business
centre in town and get a fax off for fresh ones
and then when I came back the gerbil had
somehow" – Mum glanced at me – "got out

and gone so far up the chimney that we…"

"You haven't brought it! Loretta's allergic!" cried Sarah.

"Of course not," said Mum. "Mrs Leyton-next-door's going to look after it."

"If it ever comes down," I said.

Sarah transferred her attention to me. "Oh, God," she said. "You look like a dog's dinner."

I looked back at her just as critically. She didn't look like she was supposed to – not a bit like Jaz, Jan or Jo in *Girls Upstairs*. She had on a boring old grey suit that was her shop outfit – she was the manager of the china and glass department in a big store.

"This is my latest gear," I said, looking down at myself admiringly. "Baggy shirt over Lycra cycling shorts with silver Doc Martens."

"Well, let me tell you, it looks grotesque," said Sarah, "especially those boots." She screwed up her face and turned away. "I don't know how I'm going to cope with her here, I really don't," she muttered.

"Darling," Mum said, "I wouldn't ask you unless I was desperate. And she's no trouble." Her voice faded a little. "Not really…"

"I know her, Mum. Remember?"

"And she's been so looking forward to coming. The things she's got planned."

Sarah rolled her eyes.

Mum went on. "It's just that what with this series of conferences in Europe and it being

13

the school holidays and Gran being busy..."

"And Aunty Claire being busy and Mrs Leyton-next-door being busy. Funny how they're all busy all of a sudden, isn't it? What does that tell you?"

"Shall I go in?" I asked. God, anyone would think I was a problem. I didn't take *any* looking after; the gerbil was more trouble than I was. "I'll start making myself at home, shall I?"

"No!" Mum and Sarah both shouted. And then they looked at me and added in chorus, "I really must go!"

"Don't mind me," I said, clutching my plastic bags and trying to shove my suitcase through the front door.

Sarah sighed. "Well, I'll just tell you where things are and then I've got to get back to work." She shook her head. "You're going to be bored to death here on your own, you know, and I can't possibly have time off because of the Sale and I don't know what..."

Mum flung her arms round me. "Goodbye, darling! I'll write – and ring you. And it's only ten days."

"Don't worry about me," I said, struggling to breathe through a shiny suit and two layers of perfume. "I'll be fine."

While they conspired in low voices, I slid inside and surveyed the hall. There was a big round table with some letters on it and I had a quick shifty through, but most of the envelopes were the boring brown sort with windows. Just one looked interesting – fat and white and marked *Greg Golightly: to await arrival*. The only other things in the hall were a coin box telephone and a vacuum cleaner with a sticker on it saying, *Please return immediately after use*.

I turned to see Mum pressing an envelope into Sarah's hand. "Here's something towards her keep," she said. "And a little extra inconvenience money."

"Yes, it *is* inconvenient," said Sarah. "I'm glad you appreciate that."

Mum pretended not to hear her, picked up her briefcase and slung her travel bag over her shoulder. "I'm for the tube station. Bye, darlings!"

We stood in the doorway and waved. I tried to look as if I was going to miss her, but I'm sure she wasn't fooled. Staying with Sarah in this flat was what I'd been dying to do ever since she'd moved in.

Sarah closed the front door. "Now, pest," she said. "I'm going to show you your room and leave you to it." She took my suitcase and began climbing the stairs.

"Who lives there?" I said, pointing to the door down to the basement.

"Mrs Bryant, the landlady," Sarah said. "We call her Mrs B. She's OK."

I thought of *Girls Upstairs*. "Does she listen to your problems and offer a comforting cup of tea and a slice of home-made cake when things go wrong?" I asked with interest.

"What?" Sarah said. "No, of course she doesn't."

I followed close behind her up to the first floor, noting the card pinned to the door on Flat 1: *Kevin and Mouse*. Mouse! Fancy sharing a flat with a mouse; I betted Kevin was lonely. Here, already, was someone interesting for Sarah to meet – it was going to be like in *Girls Upstairs* when Jo met Dave. Or had Sarah met him already? Had they passed in the hall, glanced longingly at each other but been too shy to speak?

On the second floor was another door and another card: *Sandy and Lyall*. Were these girls or boys or one of each?

"Do you know the people in all these flats?" I said to Sarah as we passed Flat 3: *Jules and Tasha*. "I expect you go to their parties, don't you, and borrow cups of sugar from them and climb in through their windows when you forget your key?"

"God, how you ramble on," she said, looking at me in bewilderment. "What are you talking about?"

We arrived, puffing, on the fourth floor. A small typed notice to the side of the door said: *Loretta, Sarah and Elizabeth*.

"Here we are, then," Sarah said, pushing open the door.

I went in. I knew *exactly* what it would be like.

But it wasn't.

"Is this *it*?" I said.

"What were you expecting?" said Sarah, putting down my case. "The Ritz?"

"No, but…" It was just so ordinary. It was like our sitting room at home, only more old-fashioned – a bit like Gran's. It had one settee, two armchairs, a TV, a big table and chairs, a coffee table with a phone on it, a cupboard, and a window with brown curtains. It wasn't at all like the *Girls Upstairs* flat.

"Where's the piles of newspapers and the floor cushions and the jumpers drying on bits of string?"

"What?"

"Where's the posters and the bottles with candles sticking out of them and all the mugs from the night before and the scrawled messages stuck on the walls?"

"I don't know what you're talking about," Sarah said impatiently. "This is just a flat where three working girls live – or two at the moment. Just an ordinary flat."

"It shouldn't be *ordinary*," I said. "It's girls sharing, in London, where lots of exciting things happen."

"Yeah. Tell me about it."

17

"But in my…"

"Look, I've got to go! I'm hours late and they'll have finished the Derbyshire without me."

"D'you want me to do anything?" I said, dropping the rest of my plastic bags and putting on my eager-to-please face. "I can do shopping and cleaning. Or I could cook you something – I'm really good. We did royal icing last term."

"That's useful," said Sarah.

"Maybe I could do some ironing…"

A look of alarm crossed her face. "No! Don't touch anything – especially of Loretta's. She's really fussy about her stuff. Don't you dare go in her room – she'll go mad. She wasn't all that keen on you coming here, actually."

"Why not?" I asked indignantly.

Sarah shot me a glance. "She's got a younger sister. She *knows*."

I pulled a face at the absent Loretta. "Which is my room, then?"

"You're in Elizabeth's room." She crossed behind the settee and pushed open a door. "In here."

"And where's she?"

"Moved to Edinburgh to start a new job and sort out her wedding."

"Ooh!" I squealed excitedly. "Are you going to it? Are you being a bridesmaid or anything? Who's she marrying?"

"Some sap," said Sarah dismissively.

"Has she got a long dress and…"

"Stop yapping! I've got to go!" She pointed. "Look – bathroom and loo over there, TV and video work like the ones at home. Don't touch *anything*."

"I've got to touch some things," I said reasonably. "How can I get round otherwise? I've got to touch the carpet when I walk on it."

"You know what I mean. You can do your summer homework or read a book or just sit quietly and breathe. Don't let anyone in – and remember that Mrs B's in the basement if you need her. I've told her you're coming." She took a breath. "Now, take phone messages properly – and if someone called Simon rings say I'm out and always will be."

"Who's Simon?" I asked eagerly. "Is he your boyfriend? Mum said you hadn't got one, but I knew you must have. Is he your *steady?*"

She picked up her bag. "Oh, please!"

"Is he someone you love really and you're just playing hard to get? Jan does that in *Girls Upstairs*. It usually works but you've got to be careful you don't overdo it."

"For God's sake!"

"You can tell me," I said eagerly. "I've read a lot about it. I might be able to help."

She gave an anguished scream. "If you *dare*…" She flung a black cape thing around her shoulders. "See you tonight!"

I heard the front door slam and then, smiling hugely to myself, I walked round looking at things, touching everything in sight and going in and out of Loretta's room as much as possible.

I sighed with pleasure. All day, while they were out, this was *my* flat. All mine. I looked out onto grey rooftops with plastic bags of rubbish on them. Never mind those... I was a girl who lived in London and shared a flat with two others.

I looked round. OK, so the flat didn't look like it was supposed to look, but I could change that. There were some pull-out pictures of pop stars in my magazines – I could put up those instead of the gold-framed reproduction of Somebody Famous's field of corn, and then I'd clear the mantelpiece ready for invitations to parties and start a list for messages from boyfriends.

I didn't know much about Sarah's love life. Mum thought she hadn't got one... Could Mum be right? If she was, then I was going to play Cupid. I'd be *wonderful* at it.

I smiled at the thought of greeting Sarah and Loretta after a hard day at work. I'd be capable and willing, the sort of girl who'd listen to their problems, sort them out. *"What a marvellous girl our Terri is,"* Loretta would say. *"So understanding. Far older than her years."*

"Yes," Sarah would reply fondly. *"Our little*

ray of sunshine. However did we manage with-out her?"

And maybe they'd ask me to stay on perma-nently, in Elizabeth's room, and I could go to school in London and always buy the latest gear and know what bands were in, and go to discos and clubs with them and, having taken care of their love lives, help their friends with theirs.

I frowned. It wasn't going to be that easy to find Sarah a boyfriend because she was already twenty-five, and naturally all the best men of that age would have been snapped up. I'd do my best, though. It would be a challenge.

I wandered back into Elizabeth's room – my room. I had, all to myself: a big white wardrobe, a bed with a faded pink duvet, a chest of drawers and a bedside cabinet. *Not* very exciting, true – but then I was hardly going to be in it, was I?

On the chest of drawers stood a large photo-graph of a moonfaced girl with a blonde bob, and a man with glasses. Elizabeth and the sap, I supposed. I peered at him closely – or what bits of him that weren't buried in Elizabeth's neck. He looked all right, actually – hardly sap-pish at all. Sarah was probably jealous because Elizabeth had managed to get someone to marry her and she hadn't.

I looked carefully through the clothes that Elizabeth had left in the wardrobe, but didn't fancy borrowing any so squashed them up at the end to make room for my own. I put my pants and socks and stuff in the chest of drawers and then started unpacking my plastic bags and distributing my bits around.

This done, I went into the kitchen and made myself a cup of weak tea. I sat on a chair with my feet over the back of it, marvelling at how sophisticated I must look in my new surroundings. My only regret was that none of my friends from home could see me.

I got out a selection of magazines – the ones with *Girls Upstairs* in – and read through them to refresh my memory about the sort of things that would be happening. After that I made a cheese sandwich, looked out of the window, read some more mags and watched the afternoon's soaps.

Sarah and Loretta came in together about six-thirty.

"I'm shattered!" Sarah said, throwing herself into a chair.

"Absolute nightmare," agreed Loretta, who worked at the same store as Sarah. "Bed Linen was horrendous." She cast herself onto the settee and kicked off her shoes.

"Ah–hem," I coughed, and they both looked at me.

"OK?" Sarah asked.

"This is the kid then, is it?" said Loretta. She was small and dark-haired with a pointy nose.

I decided I didn't like her.

"Terri – Loretta," said Sarah.

"Nice day?" I asked brightly.

They both groaned.

"Store was an absolute nightmare..."

"Not to mention the tube..."

"*Dreading* tomorrow..."

I smiled in a bracing way. "Are we going to a disco tonight?"

"Don't be ridiculous!" Sarah said.

"Surely she doesn't think that's what we *do*," Loretta said, giving me a pointy-nose look.

And that was the end of my first day...

2

SATURDAY

"Are you awake?" Sarah asked in a loud whisper from the bedroom door.

"No," I said, putting my head under the duvet.

"Because we're going."

I sat up. "Going where? Can I come?"

"Going to work."

"It's Saturday!"

"Shops, unfortunately, are open on Saturday," Sarah said, "and no, you can't come. Not on the first day of the Sale."

I flopped back again. "It's OK, I'll mind the flat," I said. "I'll take messages and arrange your flowers and all that."

"Yeah, you do that," said Sarah.

"And do the shopping if you like," I added.

"There's a shop round the corner," she said, "and a list in the kitchen."

A scream of anguish floated in from the sitting room. "Can't find my shoes. Absolute nightmare!"

"We're late. See you tonight!" Sarah said, going out and shutting my bedroom door behind her.

A few moments later the door was flung open again and I looked up to see Loretta standing there, scowling at me.

"Did you touch my navy linen jacket?"

I shook my head and crossed my fingers. It had been on a hanger behind her bedroom door, actually, and in a bored moment yesterday I'd tried it on. It had looked horrible and frumpy, though, and I'd taken it off quickly.

"I left it hanging on its own so it wouldn't get creased and now *someone's* buttoned it up all anyhow and the sleeves are rumpled and it looks an absolute *rag*."

I gazed at her balefully. What a fuss about nothing. In *Girls Upstairs* they wore each other's clothes all the time and no one said anything. They were pleased to lend round their clothes; they *offered* them and got quite upset if no one took them.

After a moment or two of hard staring she slammed out again. "Just like Emma ... into everything ... absolute nightmare," I heard her saying to Sarah.

I waited until they'd gone and then I got up and put the radio on really loudly. Almost immediately there was a banging from down-stairs – Jules and Tasha – and I turned the volume down because I didn't want to fall out with anyone. They might not invite us to their parties.

I had a shower and got dressed, then went into the kitchen to make a cup of tea and read the shopping list. Talk about boring! I'd assumed they'd be existing exclusively on exotic things I'd never heard of, but all the list said was: *Butter; 1 pt milk; 1 lb sausages; small sliced loaf; ¹/₂ doz eggs.*

I stared at it in disgust. I could eat all those at home! Where were the passion fruit yogurts, bottles of expensive mineral water, sunflower seeds and chocolate croissants? Honestly, these two were a dead loss. What was the point of living in London on your own if you carried on like this?

Before I went shopping I crossed Elizabeth's name from the card outside the door and added my own, then had a quick trip around the house to remind myself who was living where. I tapped on Kevin's door, ready with a rehearsed speech ("Hello! I'm staying on the fourth floor with my sister Sarah – have you met?") but Kevin wasn't in. I could hear music coming from Jules and Tasha's flat but no one answered my knock, and Sandy and Lyall were out. (Having brunch? People did that in London.)

I went upstairs to find out who lived on the fifth floor and got excited when I saw the door of the flat was open. But when I peered in there was no one there. The rooms were furnished but clearly, at present, unoccupied. I thought of *Mr Greg Golightly: to await arrival...*

Outside in the street, I walked for ages in one direction without finding anything like a shop, then turned back, past the house again, and found a grocer's on the next corner. Just beyond this were more shops, a restaurant called Pizza the Action, a stall selling vegetables and a video store.

The grocer's was self-service and I found everything on my list, plus a few extra things that I wasn't allowed to eat at home: Chocopops breakfast cereal, fudge-flavoured hot drink and a toffee apple. I also selected two broken Easter eggs.

"Hi!" I said chattily to the woman behind the till. "I'm staying just along the road, here. It's my sister's flat – I expect you know her."

"Lots of girls in flats round here."

"They use this shop," I said. "My sister's got very long fair hair and her friend's got a pointy nose. I expect they come in here a lot for party food."

"Don't think so," the woman said, adding up my purchases with a calculator. As she added, I stuffed everything in a bag.

"They're bound to shop in here," I said.

27

"They're the type who're always having little get-togethers on the spur of the moment. 'Spect they come in for … for…" I searched my mind for what the *Girls Upstairs* girls ate at parties. "French bread and exotic dips and stuff."

"We only sell white sliced, dear," the woman said. "That'll be eight pounds exactly, please."

"Eight pounds!" I juggled to pull the Easter eggs out of the bag again. "I've only got five." I smiled at her and waved the eggs. "I'll put these back on the way out."

"It's OK, I'll…" she began, but I'd already reached the shelf and had stretched up to put the eggs on it. They were bigger than I'd realized, and somehow top-heavy…

"Good job they were broken already," I called, getting out pretty smartish.

I had a quick look at the other shops, partly out of interest and partly to see if there were any Possibles for Sarah. I knew very well from *Girls Upstairs* that to spend even one evening on your own meant you were a complete and utter social disaster: I had to get Sarah a boyfriend as quickly as possible.

There was a boy on the market stall but he looked younger than me, and, in the video shop, someone rather odd with two earrings through his nose. There was also, though, doing the cooking in Pizza the Action, a droopy-moustached foreign guy… I walked back to the flat and started a Possibles list with him at the top.

I then put a clean piece of paper by the phone headed *Telephone Messages from Men!!!* and cleared a space along the mantelpiece ready for invitations. In *Girls Upstairs* they always had loads of invitations stuck behind the vases of flowers which had arrived from admirers. I hunted around for vases, but couldn't find any.

I was wondering whether to make myself a sausage sandwich when the phone rang. I put my message sheet in front of me, sat down at the table and picked up the receiver.

"Hello!" I said in a friendly and encouraging voice. "Sarah, Loretta and Terri's flat!"

"What?" came a doubtful male voice.

"Sarah, Loretta and Terri's flat!"

"Er ... is Sarah there?"

"Who is it wants her?"

"It's Simon," came the reply. And then there was a long sniff.

Simon! I thought back to what Sarah had said yesterday about him. Had she meant it about not ever being in when he phoned? Surely not.

"I'm afraid she's gone to work," I said, carefully noncommittal.

"Oh. Only I didn't see her at the station today. I thought she might have come down with that Tasmanian flu."

"It's the first day of her Sale," I said, "so I think she went in early. I'm her sister Terri, by the way. I'm staying in the flat."

"I see," said Simon. "Only there's a lot of flu about at the moment. I make sure I gargle as soon as I get in."

"Are you her boyfriend?" I asked suddenly.

He gave a self-conscious laugh. "Not ... exactly."

There was something wistful in his voice. Call it female intuition, I just *knew* he was pining for her.

"But I expect you'd like to be, wouldn't you?" I asked.

"Well, I..."

I beamed at the receiver. Of course he would! "All I'd like to say, Simon," I said, "is that faint heart never won fair lady."

"Oh," he said. There was a moment's silence and then he said, rather muffled, as if he had his hand over the phone and didn't want anyone to overhear, "Well, actually, as you're her sister... I am rather keen on her but she doesn't seem very keen on me. Rather the opposite, in fact."

I shook my head sadly.

"Well, if you ask me, Simon, she's got an unfortunate attitude towards men. That's why she's got to age twenty-five without getting married."

"Is that right?" he said, sounding interested.

"Don't lose heart, Simon. If at first you don't succeed..."

He cleared his throat anxiously. "So you recommend that I..."

"I recommend you hang on in there!" I said bracingly. "And, Simon?"

"Yes?"

"Don't forget the little touches that show you care. Chocolates, flowers..."

"Oh, I never touch flowers. Allergic to pollen, you see. Brings me out in a terrible rash."

"You could have them sent! And if not flowers, then..." I looked round the room. "A music centre or new curtains, perhaps."

"Oh, I don't think..."

"Chocolates, then," I amended hastily. "Jan in *Girls Upstairs* loves chocolates. She was right off Tom and then he sent her a box with a Persian blue kitten on and she started really fancying him."

"Oh. Right," he said in rather a puzzled voice. "Will you tell Sarah I called?"

"I will," I promised.

"And maybe I can ring you again when I feel up to it, just so you can tell me how things are going."

"Of course you can. You can ring me any time you like!" I put down the phone, well pleased with myself.

1.30 – Simon called Sarah. I wrote on my message page. *He didn't see you at station. Are you all right?* I also added him on to my list of Possibles.

Then I made a great big sausage sandwich, rearranged my bedroom furniture, watched the soaps and flicked through *Girls Upstairs* to see how often they got invited to parties. I was just getting hungry again when Sarah crashed in through the door.

She threw herself onto the settee full length. "I'm whacked!" she groaned. "China and Glass was like a battlefield."

I made sympathetic noises.

She raised her head and looked at me suspiciously. "What have you been up to?"

"Nothing," I said. I brandished my message page. It was a pity it wasn't full up, but one was better than none. "Simon rang at one-thirty."

"Oh, yes?"

I looked at her carefully for tell-tale signs of being desperately in love. She looked a bit pink but it was a bit difficult to tell if that was Love or because of the battlefield in China and Glass.

"He said he didn't see you at the station and wondered if you were ill."

She sighed heavily. It could have been a sighing-for-love sort of sigh, but possibly it was more of the fed-up, rolling eyes sort.

"He sounds *very* keen…"

"Huh."

"So I told him that he shouldn't give up, that faint heart…"

I don't think she heard what faint heart never won because my words were drowned by Loretta coming in, banging the door behind her, flinging herself into a chair and groaning twice as loudly as Sarah had.

"What an absolute nightmare! If anyone mentions the words Bed Linen I'm going to scream!"

"Never seen crowds like it!" Sarah said.

"They pushed down a display stand!"

"Four women fainted!"

"One of my assistants was attacked!"

They tried to outdo each other for a while, then fell silent. I left it a decent interval – another ten seconds or so – then asked tentatively. "Er… Are we going out tonight?"

No one said anything, but from out of nowhere a cushion landed on me.

I shook my head sadly, with a certain amount of disbelief. Saturday night – *Saturday night* – and we were staying in! Talk about social outcasts! And they were making no effort at all. I didn't know why they didn't go round to the local convent, knock at the door and ask to be taken in.

After a moment Loretta got to her feet. "I suppose I'd better get myself sorted out," she said.

I sat up straight. Don't tell me she had a date and my sister hadn't! "Are you going out with someone?" I asked.

33

"As a matter of fact, and if you must know," she said, "I'm going to stay over my mum and dad's for the night."

She charged about putting things in a bag and *absolute nightmaring* all over the place, and then she went on and on about me not even breathing in the general direction of her room, much less daring to step over the threshold. Honestly, I don't know what she thought she had in there that would interest *me*.

When she'd gone I smiled at Sarah in a bracing way. "Don't be too upset about staying in tonight."

"I'm not," she said.

I thought of Kevin downstairs. "What about throwing an impromptu fondue party?" I said. "We could ask Kevin. He's only got that little mouse for company; I bet he'd love to come."

Sarah shot me a puzzled look. "We don't possess a fondue set," she said, "and anyway, Mouse isn't exactly little."

"Well, size hardly matters, does it? The main thing is the poor man's on his own and…"

"No one could be lonely with Mouse; she's six feet tall and nearly as wide. And *noisy*. You can hear her laugh two streets away. That's why she's called Mouse. She's like an elephant."

"Oh," I said, and was glad I hadn't mucked up the Possibles list by putting on Kevin. And thinking of the list made me think of Droopy Moustache around the corner. "If you like, we could pop round for a pizza."

"The sausages will do, thanks."

I pulled a face to myself. I'd had six in my very large sandwich, leaving two. I changed tack. "Simon sounds *very* nice."

"Simon," she said out of the corner of her mouth, "is a dog biscuit."

"What's that mean? Is that good or bad?"

"It means that he's got about as much personality as a floor mop."

I tutted. "Sarah, playing hard to get is all very well, you know, but as I tried to tell you yesterday, Jan in *Girls Upstairs* tried it once too often and it all went wrong."

She sat up and looked at me in amazement. "What *are* you talking about?"

"Just that … well, at your age you can't afford to take too many chances, can you?"

She looked at me, groaned and rolled her eyes. "When are you going home?"

"Oh, not for ages yet," I reassured her.

I was going to bring True Love into her life even if I had to drag it in by the ears…

3

SUNDAY

"Cup of tea?" I asked Sarah, putting my head round her bedroom door.

"Wasstime?" she mumbled.

"Nine o'clock."

She groaned loudly. "It's Sunday! Go away!"

I retreated into my room with her cup of tea as well as my own, and picked up a pile of mags to read.

I don't mind how many times I read some of the love stories, especially the ones where the heroine is desperate to get back her ex-boyfriend, who's gone off with her best friend, and things keep happening which make you think she never will, and then in the last line he comes round and says it was all a mistake, he loves *her* really and can't live another moment without her. Those are my favourites – and I don't even care if secretly you know right from the beginning that she'll get him back.

When I'd read about twenty mags and it felt as if hours and hours had gone by, I got dressed, went out of the flat and had a bit of a prowl round the house to see if anyone was about. Some newspapers had arrived downstairs and I arranged these on the hall table, then shuffled through the brown envelopes and held the *Mr Greg Golightly* one up in case any writing showed through. I did this very slowly, looking round all the time for other possible excitements. Time was slipping by – Mum would already be on her second conference – and I hadn't even *started* trapping anyone for Sarah.

I was on my way upstairs again when someone put a hand through the banisters and grabbed my leg.

"Hello, ducks!"

I jumped. There was a little old lady grinning at me and holding onto my ankle. She was a very brightly-coloured little old lady, wearing a huge flowery caftan thing and, over it, a fringed shawl embroidered with peacocks in clashing colours.

"I'm Mrs B – from the basement," she said.

"I'm Terri," I said. "I'm staying with my sister Sarah in Sarah and Loretta and Elizabeth's flat. But Elizabeth's gone away to arrange her wedding."

"So she has," said Mrs B. "And are you enjoying yourself?"

"Well," I said consideringly, "I think I am. Only there's not much going on here, is there? I thought there would be lots of parties and things, seeing as it's London. It's not quite what I expected."

She beckoned. "You come downstairs and have a chat with me."

I went, of course. Her flat was about the same size as Sarah's and the same way round; the only difference was that it was half underground, so when you looked out of the window you just saw the railings and people's legs and feet instead of their heads. The other big difference was the furniture. Mrs B's flat was crammed with tables and chairs – easy chairs, armchairs, upright chairs, fireside chairs and a rocking chair. The tables were all piled on each other; coffee tables on dining tables, small round tables stuck upside down on kitchen tables and even a table with one leg missing, held up by a stack of paperbacks. Sarah had told me that Mrs B never threw anything away; as her tenants came and went, leaving their own odd bits of furniture behind them, she moved things downstairs in case, one day, someone moved out and took all *her* furniture with them. Judging by the caftan, the shawl and the two chiffon scarfs in lime green and orange tied round her head, I thought she must do the same with any clothes left behind, too.

"Sit yourself down," she said, pointing to five chairs at once, "and tell me why you're disappointed."

I squeezed myself past a pile of tables and into a fireside chair with three lace headrest things on it.

"It's not what I expected," I said, "because there's this serial in my magazine..." and I told her about *Girls Upstairs* with its parties and romances and heartbreaks and loves at first sight.

"Every week someone is desperately and horribly heartbroken and will never get over it," I said earnestly. "It's really lovely."

"It used to be like that here," Mrs B said when I'd finished. "Used to be what they called 'swinging'. We had sports cars arriving for my young ladies all the time and parties and people going on secret assignations or deciding to climb out of windows and run away together. But now all anyone does is go to work. Not very interesting for me, it isn't." She patted the pile of paperbacks next to her chair. "That's why I read these," she said. "As long as I've got my True Romances, true romance is never dead."

I leaned over and picked a couple of books off the pile. One was called *One Night of Love* and showed a couple wearing evening dress dancing under a palm tree, the other was

Tomorrow Too Late! and featured a girl sitting beside a palm tree wiping away a tear and looking out to sea.

Mrs B made me a cup of coffee and I decided to have it black. I'd noticed that Loretta had hers like that.

"I'm going to try and change things while I'm here," I said. "I want to show my sister what she's missing. I mean, she stayed in last night – *Saturday night!*"

Mrs B shook her head sadly. "Never would have happened in the old days. Never happens in my books. They go to balls in my books. Hunt balls and charity balls and country house balls." Her eyes gleamed. "They kiss in the shrubbery and canoodle in the conservatory."

"Sarah would like to do things like that! She'd like to meet someone and have a whirlwind romance under a palm tree, I know she would. She's just so busy working that she's forgotten what she's *supposed* to be doing. I reckon it's up to me to help her."

Mrs B beamed. "That's right. You do your good deed – trap her a nice young man. And make sure you come and tell me how you're getting on."

"Well," I said, trying not to pull a face at the taste of my black coffee. "I've already got a couple of Possibles lined up." I told her about Simon and Droopy Moustache. "And I thought I'd have a look at who else is in the house, too."

Mrs B shook her head. "All couples," she said. "Nothing doing there."

"What – Sandy and Lyall *and* Jules and Tasha?"

She nodded and then a sudden glimmer of excitement showed on her face. "Wait a minute – we've got a single gentleman moving in on the fifth floor tomorrow. Greg Golightly, his name is."

"I've seen his letter!"

"Very presentable. Paid two months in advance. And..." she paused for effect, "he's an actor! Make a lovely catch for your sister."

As we looked at each other gleefully I visualized myself at previews, meeting stars. At school I'd be able to say, casually, "My sister's boyfriend is Greg Golightly, the actor," and "I see Greg Golightly's up for another Oscar."

"I'll do it! I'll get them together!" I said. "Leave it to me."

When I went back upstairs, Sarah was still asleep – or pretending to be. And she was still asleep when someone rang at 11 o'clock.

It was a deep, male voice, asking for Loretta. I quickly got my *Messages from Men* sheet, told him Loretta was at her parents' for the day, and asked if he'd like to speak to *anyone else* instead.

"Well, who are *you*?" he asked, and I explained.

"Sarah didn't say anything about you," he said. "Terri, eh? Short for Teresa. And are you as lovely as your sister?"

"Probably," I said, not actually thinking that she *was* terribly lovely.

"And are you alike in other ways? What sort of things do you enjoy doing, Terri?"

"Oh. Listening to bands and shopping and all that," I said, then added, "and going to clubs and concerts and discos in London." Well, I would like them, if somebody took me.

"You sound rather interesting, Terri. A new girl in the flat, eh? Like a breath of fresh air. I'll have to come round and see you. Staying for long, are you?"

"Just ten days. I've got to be back by the beginning of September."

"Why's that then, Terri?" he asked. "Zooming off with the other jet-setters to Mozambique, are you? Start of the season in Monte Carlo, is it?"

"No," I said. "That's when school starts."

There was a sudden silence, then he cleared his throat. "I see," he said. "Ha ha. School, eh? Jolly good."

"Will you be calling for Loretta tonight then?" I asked eagerly.

"Er ... no. We'll meet out. Tell her Brett will see her around seven." He hung up.

I filled in the *Messages* form and then crashed around the place and put records on and in the end Sarah got up.

"Someone called Brett phoned for Loretta," I said importantly. "He sounded quite nice."

"Ah-huh," she said.

"Is he her boyfriend?"

Sarah shrugged. "I suppose you could call him that."

"Has she been going out with him long? Was it love at first sight? Is it serious?"

"I shouldn't think so," said Sarah in an irritated voice. "Why all the interest?"

I gave her a knowing yet sympathetic smile. Of course she was scratchy – it must be awful to have all your friends getting paired off while you were mouldering on the shelf. "It doesn't mean you're not going to find someone," I said comfortingly. "True Love could blossom where you least expect it. Simon might turn out to be the one for you."

She made a faint screaming sound.

"Or someone else. Someone with a moustache, perhaps... Or even an actor."

"What?! What on earth are you talking about?"

I smiled mysteriously. "Oh, nothing. Just thinking aloud."

"What did Brett say, anyway?"

"Just that he'd meet Loretta tonight about seven."

She gave a hollow laugh. "*If* he turns up."

"Is he not very reliable?" I said, glad she was

confiding in me at last. "There was someone in *Girls Upstairs* like that. His name was Jeremy and he drove all the girls mad but in the end he settled down and asked the girl in the flat below to go to Dorset with him and start a riding stable."

Sarah made a snorting noise. "Well, it might be like that in your fairy stories but let me tell you that Brett Hargreaves is definitely *not* the settling-down-and-opening-a-stables kind."

"Maybe he only seems like that because he hasn't found true love," I said wisely.

"Well, he's certainly having a good search," Sarah said. "Elizabeth saw him first, then I went out with him a few times, and now Loretta is—"

"You!" I said, thunderstruck. "*You* used to go out with him!" I stared at her open-mouthed. So that was why she was so bitter and twisted. Of course! She loved Brett and he'd been stolen from her! Now she was caught in an eternal triangle. The wallflower; the gooseberry, destined to see Brett and yearn for him, but never to get close again.

I was about to offer consoling words and information on how Jaz, Jan and Jo coped with that sort of situation when the phone rang.

"Someone asking you out for Sunday brunch!" I said, springing up and grabbing my *Messages from Men* at the same time. "Smoked salmon and scrambled eggs!"

"Sarah, Loretta and Terri's flat!" I trilled.

"Terri! How are you getting on, darling?" Mum asked.

"Fine," I said. I put down my piece of paper, disappointed.

"Being a good girl?"

I pulled an anguished face. "Yes, Mum." Fat chance of being anything else.

"Let me talk to her," Sarah said urgently, and thinking she might want to tell Mum about the latest call from Brett and how she was feeling, I dutifully handed over the phone.

Of course, it wasn't that at all. What they talked about was whether or not Mum wanted to buy a dinner service in the sale, and if so, whether she wanted two vegetable dishes or three and whether the sauce boat was a good buy. It went on so long and was so boring that I wandered into the kitchen and had eaten three pieces of toast by the time they'd finished.

"About Brett…" I said to Sarah gently when Mum had rung off. "Was there anything..?"

"I don't want to talk about him!" she snapped.

I pursed my lips. Exactly as I thought.

The rest of the day was spent tidying, cleaning, washing and ironing. I'd hoped that doing the washing might be a good way for Sarah to meet a man, because in my mags exciting things were always happening in launderettes. In *Girls Upstairs* Jan had her cousin Chelsea

staying, and Chelsea had gone to the launderette and come home with the wrong washing (a bundle of rugby shirts instead of pale
pink silk underwear – don't ask me how she
didn't realize) and then the real owner, Luke,
had come round to collect the shirts and invite
her to a party. This was just the start: a couple
of weeks later a glowing Chelsea reported to
Jan that she and Luke had set up in a flat
together and purchased their own front loader.

But I'd reckoned without Sarah's having a
washing machine of her own. The launderette
path to True Love was closed.

Late in the afternoon she decided we ought
to have some fresh air, so we went for a walk
to the park. There were quite a lot of couples
strolling arm in arm and I tried to divert
Sarah's attention from them in case she got
morbid. I also noticed that there were a lot of
single men with dogs.

"Have you ... er ... thought of getting a dog
at all?" I asked, as we walked across the grass.

She sidestepped a poo. "What on earth for?"

"For company," I said. "And also it's a good
way of meeting people. In *Girls Upstairs* one
week, Jo was without a boyfriend and so she
borrowed a dog and went for a walk across a
common and her dog made friends with
another dog and this dog's owner came up and
spoke to her dog and..."

"Stop! Stop!" said Sarah. "It all sounds

much too complicated. And I really can't see the point of keeping a dog just on the off chance that you might meet someone else with a dog."

"Well, there you are," I said. "That sums you up; you just won't make the effort, will you? Why—"

"And Mrs B doesn't allow dogs," Sarah interrupted. "So that's that."

What you might call the highlight of my day was being sent out for a pizza. At first, thinking of Droopy Moustache, I tried to persuade Sarah that we should eat there, but she said she couldn't be bothered and what was the point of having me around if I wasn't going to run errands for her?

I then decided it might actually be better to go on my own. As Sarah had turned out to be so absolutely useless at this boyfriend business it might be as well if I did the groundwork.

The trouble was, Droopy Moustache wasn't serving, so I couldn't speak to him: there was a girl behind the counter who took the orders, and he was just the person who sprinkled on the cheese and got the pizzas in and out of the ovens. The only thing I could do was talk to the girl and hope he'd overhear.

"I'm staying with my sister in a flat round the corner!" I said loudly, having placed our order for a family-sized with chilli.

"Oh, yes?" said the girl.

"I expect you've seen her in here with her flatmate. She's got long fair hair." I braced myself and added, even more loudly, "Very pretty!"

"Uh-huh?"

"The other one's got a pointy nose."

"You don't say."

"Oh, yes, Sarah's always in here buying pizzas." I smiled conspiratorially and nodded towards Droopy Moustache. "Sometimes I wonder what the attraction is, if you see what I mean…"

The girl looked at me, startled.

"She would have come in here tonight," I went on, "but I said to her, maybe you've been overdoing it. It wouldn't do to frighten him off, would it?"

"Er … no," the girl said.

Droopy Moustache got our pizza out of the oven with a shovel thing and landed it on the counter. "Itsa ready," he said.

"Itsa for my sister," I said quickly before he turned away. "Long fair hair. Very pretty."

I don't know whether he heard me or not. "I expect she'll be in here soon," I added. "*Loves* the way you sprinkle cheese!"

4

MONDAY

"I'm not sure that I want another pizza," Sarah grumbled as I hurried her along the road towards Pizza the Action. "We had one only last night."

"It's different when you're eating there," I said. "Fresher and everything. They taste better."

"D'you think so?"

"And as Loretta's coming in late and then eating with Brett…"

"We can't be too long," Sarah said as I pushed the door open. "I'm going out with a friend from work later."

"Never mind about friends from work," I said, "you can see them all day. You should be concentrating on finding yourself a nice boyfriend."

She gave me a withering look and I ignored

it and sat down at the table nearest the counter.

"This is right by the door," she said. "It'll be draughty."

"I thought you liked fresh air," I said. "It's what you wanted yesterday." As I spoke I glanced anxiously over the top of the counter. He was there all right; moustache drooping and sweat dripping from his brow. Standing in front of the big oven like that with red face and rolled up sleeves he could easily have been an engine driver or a blacksmith – something really romantic – instead of just a cheese-scatterer.

"He's a bit of all right," I said, kicking Sarah under the table and nodding towards him.

"Mmm?" she said. "D'you want chilli again? I think I'll have ham and pineapple."

"I always think men with those moustaches look so ... so interestingly foreign," I said. "Dashing and mysterious."

She stared at the menu. "Shall we go mad and have garlic bread?"

"Better not," I said, "in case you have to kiss someone later."

We ordered our pizzas and then Sarah rambled on about work and how busy they were and I interrupted and talked about moustaches. I added that it might just be my imagination but the owner of the one behind the counter kept looking at us.

"Well, at you, actually," I amended. "I think he's got the hots for you."

She pulled a face. "What on earth does *that* mean?" She got up to go to the loo.

I was quite pleased she went, actually, because while she was still gone our order arrived and I had a wonderful idea. It was a daringly brilliant *Girls Upstairs* sort of idea, and if I was quick I might just get away with it...

I nipped round to her side of the table, took up her knife and made a few deft cuts into her pizza, transforming it from an ordinary round one into a romantic heart-shaped one.

I gulped down the trimmings and a few extra pineapple chunks and got back to my own side of the table just in time.

"What on earth's this?" said Sarah, staring.

"Sit down, sit down, you'll embarrass him!" I hissed.

She sat. "Who's been messing around with my food? It looks as if a dog's been at it!"

"Ssh!" I crossed my fingers. "I think it was that man behind the counter. He brought it over and didn't say anything, but – " I remembered a phrase from a recent mag "– his eyes spoke volumes."

"He ate some of my pizza! What – was he hungry or something?"

"Of course he didn't eat it! He crafted it into a heart."

"That's not a heart!" she scoffed. "It's a rugby ball!"

I spoke in a low, meaningful voice. "It's a very beautiful idea. He's Italian, he can't speak English, so he spoke to you the only way he knew how."

"By butchering my pizza!?"

"By fashioning it into a token of love."

"I'm going to complain!"

She pushed her chair back ready to stand up and I quickly whipped her pizza away and replaced it with mine. "Don't do that," I said. "You'll upset him. They're temperamental, these Latin types. He'll probably burst into tears all over the cheese."

She glowered at me. "I can't quite believe this. I've never heard of anything so ridiculous in my life."

"Mysterious are the ways of the heart," I said wisely.

She turned her glower on the man himself. "I've a good mind to…"

"Leave it," I said. "Eat mine. Love works in funny ways – he just did it so you'd notice him."

"I've noticed him all right. He's jolly lucky that I'm in too much of a hurry to take this further."

I breathed again, relieved that she wasn't going to go and make a fuss. We both started eating. Everything seemed to be going all right and I was about to remind her that she'd always wanted to go to Italy on holiday when two things happened. First, a smiling, dark-haired woman came through the door and said "Paulo!"; second, three small children ran behind the counter, calling "Papa!"

"Oh," I said.

"Typical!" Sarah snorted.

I gulped. How was I supposed to have known? He hadn't looked like a family man. Mentally I crossed Droopy Moustache off my Possibles list.

When we got home, Loretta still wasn't in. Sarah took herself off to the bathroom to get ready to go out again and I'd just switched on the TV to catch up with the soaps when some-one rang our bell.

"I'll go!" I shouted, then ran out and right downstairs, opened the door and goggled at the really hunky James Bondish sort of man standing on the step. He was tall, dark-haired, and had an open-necked shirt with lots of manly chest hair showing. All in all, he looked like an aftershave ad come to life.

"I'm Brett," he said. "And you're er ... the kid, are you?"

"I'm Terri," I said, willingly forgiving him. As I stared, I tried to stop my jaw from drop-ping. So this was Brett. No wonder Sarah was bitter and twisted about losing him. I opened the door wider.

"Enjoying yourself up here, are you?" he asked, coming past and patting me on the head. He looked at me a bit uneasily. "Ha ha. You sound a lot older on the phone, anyone ever tell you that?"

"Loretta's not in yet," I said breathlessly. "Sarah's in the shower."

He started up the stairs. "That's OK. I'll wait!"

Back in the flat, I rushed to my room, grabbed the Possibles list, wrote in the name Brett with two stars beside it, and rushed out again.

I sat down next to him on the settee. "I don't know what time Loretta's due in," I said. "Were you off anywhere special?"

"We were just going to grab a bite and then go to the movies," he said. "I want to see that new horror one, *Revenge of the Killer Bunny* or whatever it's called."

"Fancy," I said, then thinking that here was a golden opportunity, added, "Sarah loves horror films. She was saying only the other day she was desperate to see that one."

"Really?" said Brett. "I didn't think she was keen on them. When we were going around together she'd never come and see anything I liked."

"Oh, she's changed since then!" I exclaimed. "Realized the error of her ways..." I hoped I was implying that she'd made a terrible mistake both in passing up on horror films and in passing up on him.

He raised his eyebrows.

I scuttled off to the bathroom. "It's Brett," I hissed through the door at Sarah. "Make yourself look beautiful before you come out."

"What on earth for?" she said loudly.

"Sshh! Because."

"Because what? What are you talking about?"

"Because you might still have a chance with him, of course!"

"Per-lease!"

I scuttled back.

Brett sat looking at a newspaper and I sat pretending to read a mag but actually studying him and making plans. When Sarah appeared – no make-up and an old dressing gown – I nearly died. "Sit down, Sarah! Sit there!" I said. "I'll get you and Brett a coffee, shall I?"

"Hi, Brett – no thanks," she said, sweeping through the room. "I've got to get ready to go out."

"Anywhere nice?" I asked lightly.

"I told you. Just for a drink with a friend from work."

I waited until she'd gone into her room. "She's meeting Tristram again!" I said. "He's the one with the big black sports car. He's always popping over. Always bringing her flowers!"

"Really?" said Brett, looking round for them.

"She usually gives them to hospitals," I improvised quickly. I gave a light laugh. "Too many for one girl. So generous…"

Brett looked at his watch and then stretched forward to switch on the TV.

"Don't know what time Loretta will be in," I said. I shook my head sadly. "She's not exactly reliable about timekeeping, is she?" I let my voice fade away. "Or much else, really, when it comes to it."

Brett, staring at the TV screen and not listening to me, gave a sudden hoot. "Hey! Look at her coming out of her dress!"

I looked. There was a quiz show on and one of the hostesses was twirling round in a very tight sequined number.

Brett slapped his thigh. "A guy doesn't mind paying his TV licence when he gets sights like that!" he said. "Value for money, that's what that is!"

I frowned at the screen. "Not a patch on Sarah, she isn't. Why, Sarah was just walking down the road the other day and someone came up to her from Hollywood and…"

The door was suddenly flung open. "Brett, sweetie! Sorry I'm late!" said Loretta, rushing over and pecking at him with her pointy nose. "That tube – absolute nightmare! Six District Lines in a row and never the right one!"

"Not to worry," Brett said. "Little … er …

thingy here has been entertaining me."

"Aren't you the lucky one?" said Loretta, and I may be imagining things, but I thought I could detect a whiff of sarcasm.

She pointed her nose in my direction and raised her eyebrows so that they disappeared underneath her fringe. "Don't let us keep you, Terri. Haven't you got comics to read in your room?"

"Not really," I said.

Later, much later, when everyone had gone out and I was just thinking about having a monster bubble bath and using all their oils and potions and things, I heard a crashing noise and some voices outside.

"I say!" a man's voice said. "I'm never going to get this blasted thing up these stairs."

I dashed to the door and pressed my ear against it.

"Of course you will, Mr Golightly," came the soothing voice of Mrs B. "Just hoist it above your head and twist it round the corner."

I stuffed my T-shirt back into my jeans: Mr Greg Golightly To Await Arrival had arrived!

Another crash – when I peeped out there he was, sitting on the floor with a large trunk on top of him.

Mrs B, wearing a pink sparkly jumper under what looked like a school pinafore dress, beckoned me out. "Terri is staying with her sister

Sarah for a week or so," she announced. "Terri, this is Mr Golightly."

Greg Golightly was quite small – but taller than Sarah, thank goodness – and was wearing designer jeans with a checked shirt. Trendy, yet somehow sporty, I thought approvingly.

He pushed the trunk off and sprang to his feet. "Don't tell me, young lady – you've seen me before!"

I looked at him consideringly and realized that yes, I had, though I couldn't think where.

"Mouthwash ad!" said Greg Golightly. "I was the germ who lingered too long and got swept away by a rose-pink wave of Rins-away!"

"And what about Mr Brock the Busy Badger?" prompted Mrs B.

"You might not actually recognize my face from that series," Greg Golightly said, "because I was wearing a furry face. But I bet you remember this…" He put his head on one side, flung his arms wide and started sidestepping jauntily.

> I'm Brock, I'm Brock,
> I work around the clock,
> First you see me, then I'm gone,
> I'm Brock, I'm Brock, I'm Brock!

Mrs B and I burst into applause.
He bowed.

"I've definitely seen you!" I said. "I remember the dance."

"Ah, Golightly by name and Golightly by nature!" he said.

"You'll have to come and show it to my sister. She loves badgers!"

"I am always happy," he said solemnly, "to meet a fan. I never forget that without my fans, I'd be nowhere."

"Well, quite so," said Mrs B.

Greg Golightly bent over the trunk once again and, not wanting to get involved in any fetching and carrying, I wished him a pleasant moving in, said if he was having a flat-warming to be sure to remember us, and went back inside.

I went to my room, crossed Droopy Moustache off my list and put Greg Golightly on it. With three stars.

After that, humming *There's No Business Like Show Business*, I ran a bath.

5

TUESDAY

"Can't you just go up and look at him?" I pleaded to Sarah the following evening. "Give him a quick once-over and see what you think."

"What on earth for?"

We were in the kitchen and she was doing what she called, "Giving the cooker a birthday", although if anyone had given me a birthday treat by scouring me with wire wool I don't think I'd have been pleased.

"Because he's really nice. An actor. Almost famous," I said.

"In theatre or TV?" she asked.

I looked at her from out of the corner of my eye, trying to judge which would make him more interesting to her. "Both," I said. I began to hum the "Busy Mr Brock" song. "Er ... do you like wildlife, Sarah?"

"I thought," she said, smirking, "that you were trying to fix me up with a man, not a squirrel."

"But badgers are lovely creatures, aren't they?" I mused. "So sort of ... badgery. So very ... er ... black and white."

She lifted out the grill tray and a shower of breadcrumbs hit the floor.

"Sarah," I said, going for the hard sell, "this could be your big chance. Play your cards right and you could be attending TV quiz shows all the time. Not to mention getting free bottles of mouthwash."

"What?!"

I sighed. "They never do things like clean cookers in *Girls Upstairs*," I said. "Do stop and come upstairs and look..."

Before she had time to reply Loretta charged into the kitchen and grabbed the mug of black coffee which Sarah had left on the side for her.

"Absolute nightmare. Brett's coming at seven and I'm not nearly ready." She looked at me. "What's that you were saying about someone moving in upstairs?"

I clamped my lips together and shrugged.

Across the hotplate Sarah gave me a nasty look, so grudgingly I said, "Oh, just some ole bloke. No one interesting. Not an actor in designer jeans or anyone."

"Oh," Loretta said. She tossed her head back, put her pointy nose in the air and moved off to the bathroom. There followed a short scream, and she reappeared. "My bottle of Madame de Pompadour bath oil is empty. Absolutely empty! Not a drop in it!"

They both looked at me. "Maybe it evaporated," I said.

Loretta narrowed her eyes. "Or maybe someone was rather over generous with it ... someone not too far away from where I'm standing."

She went out again and I looked indignantly at Sarah. "That's not very nice – talking to you like that, is it? Making accusations."

"I don't think it was me she meant," Sarah said severely. "Terri, you really mustn't take other people's stuff without asking."

"I was borrowing," I said. "Girls always borrow in flats. They're forever taking each other's tights and shampoos and hair sprays. They insist on lending each other their best dresses. Besides, no one was here to ask." Humming again, I poured hot water into a mug to make a black coffee.

Sarah looked at me, then the coffee. "You hate your coffee like that," she said.

"As a matter of fact," I replied, "I quite like it. It just shows that I'm a lot more sophisticated than you thought, doesn't it?"

I took a sip, and, as her head had now disappeared right into the cooker, poured half of it down the sink. "So will you go upstairs and look at him, then?"

"What? Of course I won't! Don't be so ridiculous. How can I just go and view a man? He's not a painting on public display."

Loretta ran out of the bathroom swathed in a satin dressing gown and I looked at her with interest. "Not another absolute disaster, I hope?"

She made a *Grrr* sort of noise. "Where's my Antoinette de Valois moisturizing pre-bath lotion?!"

I picked up the bottle from beside the sink. "Is this it?"

"You've been using it!" she said in an out-raged voice.

"I just used the tiniest bit to oil the fridge door. It was squeaking."

"Terri!" exclaimed Sarah.

"Well, really!" said Loretta.

"I thought you'd be pleased," I said, and added, "It doesn't squeak any more," as Loretta rushed out again with the bottle.

Sarah resumed scraping and scouring.

"Are Loretta and Brett going somewhere nice?" I asked, pouring a little more black coffee down the sink.

"To the opening of a new restaurant in the West End," Sarah said.

"An opening!" I breathed. "There'll be stars there, won't there?"

"I daresay." More scouring noises.

"They'll have pink champagne and tara-masalata – what *is* taramasalata? – and if you were still going out with Brett it could be you going."

She made a snorting noise.

"And maybe he would have asked me to go along, too." I became wistful. "I'd like to go somewhere…"

Sarah sighed. "I suppose I'd better take you out. I promised Mum. OK, we'll go out tomorrow night."

"Great!" I said. "I can wear my silver DMs." I bent towards the cooker, my voice dripping with sympathy and understanding. "You know, it may not be too late for you and Brett. You're much nicer than Loretta and I reckon that if I just dropped a few hints about you wanting him back it might do the trick. It would at least make him think…"

Sarah emerged from the cooker and advanced towards me waving the scouring pad and almost breathing fire. "Don't you dare," she said. "If you ever dare to say one word to Brett about me I'll get hold of you and tear you to pieces with my bare hands."

I escaped into the sitting room, reflecting that it really was true that hell had no fury like a woman scorned. I'd have to be very careful where Brett was concerned; very careful indeed. *Subtle* was my key word, I decided.

I was lounging about in the sitting room,

reminding myself (by reading about it) that True Love wasn't really dead – when the phone rang.

"If that's Brett, say I'm running late!" Loretta screamed.

"If that's Simon say I'm out!" called Sarah. I picked up my message form. It was Simon.

"Is Sarah there?" he asked, in the sort of voice which implied that he rather thought she wouldn't be.

"I'm really sorry," I said, "she's under the c– weather. Under the weather. Not at all well."

"I've had a bit of a nasty head cold myself, actually," he said. "Felt rather faint on the bus. Had to have two aspirin and a lie down when I got in."

"Oh, dear."

"Of course, I have got a weakness. As soon as I get a cold it goes to my head. Or my stomach." He hesitated. "Is Sarah too ill to come to the phone?"

"Hang on," I said. I tiptoed into the kitchen and whispered, "Simon wants to speak to you. He sounds a bit weak – I think he's fading away out of love."

"Good riddance," said Sarah, and I gave her a cold stare. Heartless or what?

I tiptoed back. "I'm afraid she's much too weak to hold the phone."

He sighed. "I hardly see her these days.

What with that and my vulnerability when it comes to germs, I'm not doing too well." He tutted sadly. "Perhaps it's my biorhythms."

I turned away from the kitchen so that Sarah wouldn't hear. "She does like you, Simon," I said. "Only yesterday she called you a biscuit – a d— a … a *chocolate* biscuit. But if you don't mind my saying so, you really ought to try to be a bit more manly. And remember what I told you about flowers and things."

"Ah, yes. Flowers and chocolates."

"The way to a woman's heart," I whispered. "In *Girls Upstairs* Rupert sent Jaz a huge bunch of roses all wrapped in pink paper; enough for every vase in the house. She thought she was going off him, but when she saw the flowers she changed her mind."

A timid sniff came down the line.

"So I'll give Sarah your love, shall I?"

"Yes, please."

"When she's well enough to receive it, of course." I put down the phone quickly so that he shouldn't hear her warbling happily in the kitchen.

I sat for a while looking through back numbers of my magazines and thinking deeply, and a bit later, when Sarah had finished birthdaying the cooker, I casually asked if she'd like me to make her a sandwich and a cup of coffee. Earlier she'd said she didn't know what she fancied for supper – and of course I didn't dare utter the word *pizza*.

"That would be nice," she said, sounding surprised.

She was curled up with her feet under her, reading a book and picking black bits of cooker off her T-shirt. I looked at her critically; for the scene I had in mind I'd have preferred her on a swing wearing a floaty dress, with flowers in her hair, but she'd just have to do.

I went into the kitchen and put the kettle on, then looked for the sugar jar. It was about a quarter full, and I carefully emptied it into the bin, shaking the plastic liner a bit so that all the evidence went to the bottom. I then told Sarah that we were right out.

"I don't mind my coffee unsugared," said Sarah.

"That's all right," I said, smiling brightly. "I'll go and get some."

"Where from? Don't be ridiculous. I can quite easily manage without."

"No. I insist. You've been working so hard…" And I grabbed a cup, disappeared out of the flat and was up the stairs like lightning.

When Greg Golightly opened his door, he was holding a bundle of papers in his hand and wearing a harassed expression.

He passed a hand across his brow. "Rehearsals … auditions … play readings…" he said in a faint voice. "So many lines, so little time."

I smiled an apologetic smile and pushed my cup under his nose. "I'm so sorry, could I possibly borrow some sugar? It's for my sister. She's been working really hard cleaning the flat – the girl she lives with doesn't lift a finger – and I said I'd make her a coffee."

"But of course!" he flung the script – I presumed that's what it was – behind him onto a table. "One must never be too busy for one's public! Now, I presume you want the white and not the brown?" he went on. "Or would you like the coloured cocktail crystals?"

"If that's the sort that looks like little coloured rocks – yes, please!" I said.

He came out of the kitchen. "I'll give you a whole cupful, then you can replace it."

"That's right," I said. I knew the form. Jaz, Jan and Jo were always borrowing sugar from men in other flats. You had to return it a day or so later, and then the man invited you in, and then you casually asked him round ("Oh, we're having a few friends in tomorrow…") and after that it was all down to choosing the colour of your bridesmaids' dresses.

I went to take the cup from Greg and instantly sort of doubled up, clutching one hand inside the other. "Agghh!"

"I say! Something wrong?" he asked in concern.

"My hands! They find it difficult to hold things." I hesitated, biting my lip. "I suppose you couldn't ... carry the cup downstairs, could you? My sister is dying to meet you, by the way."

"Really," he murmured. "One's public ... well, of course..."

I clattered downstairs, chatting all the way so that he couldn't change his mind. "My sister – Sarah, her name is – has been terribly busy socializing or she would have called on you herself. She was saying only the other day that people who do TV adverts must be really fascinating and..."

As we reached the door of the flat, Loretta came out like a whirlwind. "Absolute nightmare. Nails wouldn't dry, hair went wrong. Absolutely hours late!" She glowered at me, flashed a smile at Greg and ran down the stairs.

Greg gazed after her in what looked suspiciously like admiration. "Was that your sister?"

"Certainly not," I said. "That's the other one. The one I told you about: pointy nose; sits around all day while my sister works her fingers to the bone."

I pushed open our door. Sarah was standing by the window looking down into the road, from where Brett could be heard revving his car and beeping his horn.

"There you are, Terri," she said. "I was looking out for you. I thought you must have gone to the shop."

I eyed her knowingly. How sad – pretending she'd been looking out for me when she'd been standing there desperate for a glimpse of Brett.

"This is Greg," I said, "from upstairs. He's lent us some sugar. Coloured cocktail crystal type."

Her jaw dropped. She'd probably never come face to face with anyone nearly famous before and didn't know how to behave. "Oh, really, Terri!" she said. "And you've made him come downstairs with it, too."

"Not at all, not at all," Greg said. "I couldn't let you go coffee-less – and on hearing of your sister's hand problem, I was only too delighted to carry the sugar myself. Besides, running up and down stairs keeps one in trim. Golightly by name, Golightly by nature, that's me!"

"Ah," said Sarah.

"Greg – this is my sister, Sarah," I announced. It was an auspicious moment; a deeply meaningful time that they might remember all their lives. It was a pity about the T-shirt with bits of cooker grease on it – and her hair was a mess – but apart from that she didn't look too bad.

I stared from one to the other. Would it be love at first sight? Would forces like electric currents pass between them when they touched?

"Sarah likes badgers," I said, backing away,

"and I'm just going to the shop. See you later!"

"Terri!" Sarah shouted after me in a screamy voice.

"If you like badgers, I expect you remember this song!" I heard Greg saying as I closed the door. And then the strains of "Brock the Busy Badger" followed me as I ran down the stairs.

6

WEDNESDAY

"Honestly," I said crossly to Mrs B the following morning, "she wasn't a bit grateful. I went to all that trouble getting him down for her, and when I went back he'd disappeared and she'd worked herself into a monstrous temper. Flew at me, she did!"

Mrs B tutted sympathetically.

"She'd got rid of him within ten seconds, she said."

"Never!"

"There he was, coloured cocktail crystals in his hand, thinking he was meeting his public – and my sister sends him off with a flea in his ear! I don't know how I'm going to get them together now!"

Mrs B shook her head and the dangly chandelier earrings she was wearing tinkled slightly. "There's just no helping some people."

"I can't understand why she's being like this. I mean, I know she wants to get married – I heard her talking to Loretta about it the other night. 'Lucky old Elizabeth, if only that was me,' she said. And then she passes up a golden opportunity to get chatted up by an actor!"

Mrs B tutted and tinkled some more.

"And then she tried to get out of taking me out tonight – but I reminded her that she'd promised."

Mrs B brightened. "Now, then. Where are you going?"

"Not sure," I said moodily.

She flourished a paperback with a picture of a couple standing on a beach under a palm tree with a cruise liner in the background. "In *Sorrento Surprise* this lonely girl goes on a cruise and ends up with proposals from six different men!"

"Mmm," I said, "I don't think I'm going to persuade Sarah to go on a cruise."

"Well, my advice is to try for a nightclub. Good places for meeting and greeting, nightclubs are. In *Dancing in Datchet* a girl has a blind date in one, and by mistake starts chatting to the wrong man. Who turns out to be the right man, if you see what I mean."

"I don't think Sarah would recognize the right man even if he came up with a label on him," I said, and sighed. I put down my hardly drunk mug of black coffee – I hadn't been able to get to the sink to pour it away – and stood up. "I'd better go," I said. "I had to promise to vacuum and dust the flat and get all the shopping."

Mrs B saw me through the maze of furniture to the door. "You have a good time out with your sister, ducks, and come and tell me about it in the morning." She winked. "Do your best – who knows what excitement you could cook up tonight!"

I went upstairs and spent the rest of the day – when I wasn't playing Cinderella – looking at my clothes and trying to decide what to wear. It all depended on where we were going, of course; Sarah hadn't actually told me, and she'd still been in half a huff when she went to work, so I hadn't dared ask.

Yes, I reflected, she was definitely a lot more bitter and twisted now than when she'd lived at home. But that's what happened, of course, when you couldn't find True Love.

She came in at six-thirty. By this time I'd had a shower (it had had to be a shower, Loretta hadn't yet replaced the bath oil) and face pack, followed by a hair wash and re-mousse. I'd also sorted out three possible outfits for me and six for Sarah. I'd found quite a decent top in one of her drawers – black and nightclubby, good for getting off with men – but when I'd ironed it, it had gone all small and shrivelled. I'd quickly put it back, under several other things, and practised saying, "Never seen it before in my life."

"Shall I run you a bath?" I asked. "Are we going to a nightclub?"

Sarah rolled her eyes and sighed. "I'd forgotten we were supposed to be going out. I'm whacked."

"You'll be all right after a bath," I said briskly, going into the bathroom and turning both taps on full, "and I've laid out several outfits for you to choose from."

A groan carried through from her bedroom. "I'm not wearing any of these! They're evening things."

I stood in the doorway, hands on hips. "Well, we're going out in the evening, aren't we?"

"Yes, but people don't wear sparkly things any more. I haven't worn these since I came to London."

"I didn't know how swish it was going to be. Aren't we going to a nightclub, then?"

"Of course we're not going to a nightclub! I don't know any nightclubs!"

That figures, I thought. "Are we going to a karaoke bar, then? We had a session at the end-of-term disco and I did six songs and I was really wild. Everyone said that I..."

"No," she said shortly. "We aren't going to a karaoke bar. I would die rather than set foot in a karaoke bar. If someone paid me a thousand pounds I wouldn't go to a karaoke bar."

I shook my head sadly. Some people just didn't know how to live. "Where are we going, then?" I asked.

"Oh, we'll just go to some wine bar or other. There's one round the corner in the high street."

"A wine bar?" I said, and then, just to get her in a good mood, added, "Is that where people sit around whining?"

"Oh, ha ha. Haven't heard that one before," said Sarah, and then, "Terri! Turn those bath taps off at once!"

An hour later we were sitting in the wine bar in the high street. I wasn't wearing my silver boots or any of the things I'd picked out – just an ordinary skirt and T-shirt. Sarah wasn't wearing anything I approved of – just some old black dress with an old white jacket over it.

I decided, nightclub or no, I was still going to do my best by her, so I looked over all the men in the place carefully, sizing up their suitability to be her boyfriends, whilst also memorizing details of the interior so I could impress my friends at school next term. "Just a little wine bar in London," I'd say. "My sister knows the owners. I often went there with her. Such a laugh!"

"D'you come in here very often?" I asked Sarah, who was studying the menu. "Do they know you?"

"Quite often," she said. "Sometimes I come in with a friend from work."

"Ever got lucky?"

She frowned, not understanding.

"Ever pulled anyone?" I elaborated.

She looked at me sharply. "What a disgusting expression." She passed over the menu. "And don't go choosing anything too expensive, either. No lobster."

I picked *lasagne verde* and resumed my study of the men, most of whom were in little groups up at the bar. Every so often something about them went bleep – their watches, their pagers or their phones – and then they'd look at the thing that had done it, frown and rush outside. The only ones sitting down eating seemed to have partners with them already, and even I didn't think I could push Sarah in anywhere and make a threesome.

All in all, it seemed like we were heading for another wasted evening. I would just have to concentrate on the three Possibles I already had on hold. But then I craned my neck to look towards the back of the room and – hurray! – there was one man on his own, sitting quietly reading a book. Quite a decent-looking man, too, from what I could see of him.

Pretending to be admiring the decor (plastic bunches of grapes growing on a plastic vine) I studied him more minutely. Decent-sized, not too fat, with fair hair and a lot of it. Glasses,

77

which meant he was short-sighted, but at her age she couldn't expect to get a perfect specimen. Anyway, the glasses, which were gold-rimmed, made him look quite brainy. I was sorry I hadn't brought the list out with me – as far as Possibles went, it was the more the merrier.

Sarah gave our order and when the waiter (too old to be worth consideration) had disappeared, I kicked her under the table.

"He's nice," I said, nodding in the direction of Brainbox.

She pursed her lips and frowned. "Terri," she said, "let's get one thing clear. I'm not interested in any of these men you keep trying to pair me up with. If you persist in this ridiculous matchmaking nonsense I shall ring Mum and tell her I can't put up with you a moment longer, and then she'll have to come home early."

I looked at her unblinkingly. "I'm only thinking of you," I said. "You lead such a sad, loveless life and you could be having such fun. Why, Jaz, Jan and Jo have a riot! They—"

She held up her hand. "Stop! I don't want to hear another word."

"OK," I said, shrugging. "If that's the way you want it, I won't bother to help you any longer." I had my fingers crossed, of course.

I watched the man all through my lasagne, while Sarah was wittering on about work and china and glass and managers and so on. My mind wrestled with the problem of how to get him and Sarah together. What would the *Girls Upstairs* girls have done? Gone past him and tipped a bowl of soup into his lap, probably. They were fun like that. But *I* couldn't do that. It wouldn't be – my new word – *subtle* enough.

Then I got an idea.

My chance came when Sarah went up to the bar to change her order of some French pudding to some Italian pudding I couldn't say the name of.

She started chatting to the woman serving so I quickly pencilled a note on my paper napkin between the smudges of lasagne. There wasn't time to put much, just *Please join me and my sister for a drink. Signed, the Girl in the Black Dress*. That sounded nicely mysterious, and rather more like Mrs B's romantic novels than *Girls Upstairs*. I was obviously getting more sophisticated – maybe it was all the black coffee.

I then noticed that half the women in the place had black dresses and added, *And White Jacket*, then, just to be doubly sure, *And Red Beads*.

I pretended to be heading for the loo at the end of the room and veered slightly off course to drop the napkin casually on Brainbox's open book. Next moment I was back at our table: Sarah would never know I'd been away.

"Did you want ice-cream with your apple pie?" she asked, when she came back herself.

I nodded, my heart beating fast.

"I thought you would. I've changed it from cream."

"Good. Good," I said. Would he come straight away? Would he be thrilled and intrigued? Would he, smiling hugely, say he'd love to join us for a drink but the first one was on him and how about pink champagne?

People were arriving and leaving all the time, but I didn't bother to look any more – I was staring at the plastic vines and wondering what I'd do if my note had somehow fluttered to the floor and he'd missed it. And while I was doing all this wondering, I heard an explosion of rage from his direction. I looked over – as did half the room – to see that a blonde woman in a green jacket had just arrived at his table and was standing, hands on hips, glowering, absolutely *glowering* in our direction.

"What a cheek ... thinks she can go around luring people's husbands, does she? It's not safe to leave a man sitting in a wine bar on his own now ... well, honestly!"

My toes started curling, but I gave no indication that all my insides had turned to spaghetti.

Brainbox was holding the woman's hand, trying to soothe her and make her sit down. Everyone else was staring at them, riveted.

"The hussy! I've a good mind to…"

Brainbox pulled her into her seat.

Sarah was staring along with everyone else. "Gosh," she said, looking behind her several times to see who the woman could possibly mean. "What d'you think all that was about?"

I tried to straighten my toes and my insides, assumed my blankest, most innocent expression. "Can't think," I said.

"She seemed to be staring towards *us*!"

I shook my head vehemently. "No, no! She was staring at the woman behind the bar."

"Surely not! She's old enough to be her grandmother! No one could possibly call *her* a hussy!"

"You don't know what goes on behind locked doors," I said. "Outside a little old granny – inside a temptress!"

Sarah laughed; the woman in green was quiet; my insides began to settle themselves.

Our puddings arrived, we started eating, Sarah glancing up at the woman every now and then.

"She's still looking!" she said after a couple of moments. "She's not eating her food. She's just staring over here all the time."

"Not *here*. At the woman behind the counter," I amended.

"I'm not sure that she is. The woman behind the counter isn't behind the counter now. She's on the till."

"Perhaps she's got funny eyes," I said. "There's a teacher at school like that – you think she's looking out of the window but really she's looking straight at you. Catches loads of people out. Last term she—"

"Oh, do be quiet," Sarah said. She pushed away her pudding. "I can't eat any more. That woman's putting me off – glowering at me like that." She got up. "I think I'll go and ask her what the matter is."

"Don't be silly!" I almost squealed. Then, seeing Sarah's mind was made up and knowing that drastic measures were called for, I abandoned my pudding. I made a low moaning noise. "I feel awful," I told her. "I think I might be sick!"

She seemed torn for a moment, but I made a few very suggestive noises and she sat down again.

"You're probably just tired," she said. "See – you'd never stand the pace of living in London all the time."

I yawned elaborately, covering my mouth with one hand and rubbing my tummy with the other. "It's not that," I said. "It's not just ordinary tiredness. It's sickness as well. It's that sleeping sickness!"

She rolled her eyes. "So you've been bitten by a mosquito carrying tropical sleeping sickness in South Kensington, have you?"

"Yes," I said.

Sarah shot another indignant glance over towards the woman in green, and I rolled my head onto my chest. "See! I just fell asleep then!"

"OK, OK." She stood up and, my sleeping sickness miraculously cured, I whizzed round to the till.

As Sarah got out her purse she glanced over her shoulder once more. "She's still staring. I really feel I ought to go and…"

I sagged against her. "It came over me again! I was almost sick and almost fell asleep at the same time. I was just standing there next to you and…"

"OK! We're going," said Sarah. She paid the bill and opened the door for me. "I don't know what's happened here tonight, but I can't help feeling that you've been at the bottom of it."

7

THURSDAY

"But you must admit she's got the wrong attitude towards men!" I said to Mum on the phone. "She keeps being off-putting. If she's not careful she's never going to get married!"

Mum sighed heavily. All the way from Brussels it came over as clear as anything. "Perhaps she doesn't want to. Has that occurred to you, Terri?"

"Course she does. She keeps saying how jealous she is of Elizabeth – she admits it! And she's really upset that Loretta's got Brett – you should have seen her standing at the window just staring at him." I paused. "She's eating her heart out!"

"I don't know about that," Mum said. "Why do you always have to exaggerate everything? I really can't imagine that Sarah's bothered one way or the other, so either you've got her terribly wrong, or I have."

"You have," I said.

"Look, darling, I've got to go. Please try to be good for just a few days longer – and that means not meddling in Sarah's life in any way. She won't thank you for it, you know."

"But there's this one upstairs – an actor – he's really—"

"I'll try and ring you again on Saturday – and I'll see you next Monday morning," she said hurriedly. "Bye!"

I put down the phone. Mum didn't understand, of course. Mum hadn't seen, hadn't lived with this new, crossed-in-love Sarah. When I'd trapped the right man and Sarah had found True Love, then everyone would thank me. But I only had four more days to make it all happen. I had to get things moving…

Later that day I was feeling quite bored (if I hadn't had my True Love project to work on I think I'd have been bored all the time) when the bell for our flat rang. I went downstairs and when I opened the front door a tall, thinnish man stood there holding a bunch of flowers, well wrapped up in paper, at arm's length.

"I'm Simon," he said. He sounded as if he was speaking through his nose: *I'b Sibod*. He sniffed. "And you must be Terri."

"That's right." I stared at him. He looked like a mournful bloodhound – a weedy, undernourished bloodhound with the suggestion of a drip on the end of its nose. Not much of a contender in the Hunky Boyfriend stakes.

"Do you want to come in?" I asked, screwing up my eyes a little and trying to think how he'd look in a top hat and tails. A very big top hat would be best, I decided. That way you'd hide as much of him as possible.

He shook his head. "Better not," he said, wiping his nose on a small piece of tissue. "One of us could be contagious. These germs hang about, you know." He peered behind me up the stairs. "Sarah gone to work, has she?"

I nodded. "She's got over the ... er ... whatever it was she had."

Still holding the flowers well away from him, he swung his arm towards me. "I bought her these," he said. "I asked for ones with not much pollen on but they've still made me sneeze."

"At least you made the effort," I said encouragingly, "and these – " I tore back the paper a little to see a weird, rather ugly flower I'd never seen before, "these orange pompon ones are Sarah's favourites."

"That's lucky," he said. "They were on special offer."

Oh dear, I thought. Not much of a suggestion of the extravagant, passionate gesture... "Any message, Simon?" I asked.

"Just tell her..." he frowned for a moment, obviously thinking deeply, then shrugged and looked confused.

"Leave it to me!" I said. "I'll think of something appropriate. Appropriate, yet subtle."

"All right," he said, "do your best..." And he sniffed wistfully as he went away.

Back in the flat, I tried to make the orange pompons look a bit more like a luxurious bouquet for a loved one and a bit less like a scraggy bunch that a stallholder had been desperate to get rid of. By soap-time I'd arranged and rearranged them so many times that most of the orange bits had come off. Also, in trying to make them the right length to fit into the only thing like a vase I could find, I'd cut them a bit too short. The finished effect, then, was of stumpy green twigs sticking out of a tooth mug. After much consideration, I removed a lot of the twigs and just left a few falling about at random. It looked artistic, I thought. Vaguely Japanese.

To compensate for Simon not having sent a luxurious bouquet and for his lack of enterprise regarding messages, I spent the rest of the afternoon composing a poem from him. I looked through my dictionary for help, but after much agonizing realized there wasn't a decent word to rhyme with Sarah. One I could think of that nearly went was Malaria, but somehow I didn't think that sounded very romantic. In the end I wrote:

Sare, oh, Sare,
You have beautiful hair
And a dainty little seat.
If you say that you'll be mine
I'll stand upon my feet.

I knew it wasn't quite right – what else could he stand on? – but apart from *I'll eat a piece of meat* I couldn't think of another last line.

Sarah and Loretta came in together just after six and had hysterics.

"What is *this?*" Sarah asked, prodding the twigs.

"Flowers from Simon," I said. "With all his love."

"Those are *flowers?*" Loretta asked.

"It's a Japanese arrangement," I said distantly. "They're called origami or Ikea or something."

"Do you mean ikebana?" Loretta asked sarcastically.

"I expect so," I said.

Loretta, pointed nose pointing upwards, carried the arrangement into the kitchen and stood it on the waste bin.

"And just listen to the poem!" Sarah started reading it out, her voice getting higher and more hysterical with each word. "He never wrote that!"

I snatched it back. "No, he didn't exactly write it himself," I said stiffly. "He sort of implied it and because I'm very sensitive about things like that I translated it into a poem."

Sarah groaned loudly. "For heaven's sake! You've been encouraging him, haven't you?"

"Of course she has," Loretta said. "I told you having her here would be an absolute disaster."

"I haven't done a thing," I said indignantly. "You had him before I got here!"

"Are you sure you haven't said anything to him?"

"I might have just given him a few tips about dealing with women generally ... you know, telling him what they like and all that."

"Well, you can stop telling him!"

"Or tell him that they like men who go off round the world for a very long time!" Loretta put in, and they both screeched.

"I think you're both very cruel and heartless," I said. I took the Japanese flower arrangement from the kitchen bin and put it on the windowsill.

A bit later, when I was deep in a mag, Sarah threw a cushion at me. "Have you taken that sugar back to Badger face upstairs yet?"

"No, I haven't," I said with dignity. "*You're* supposed to take it back. And then while you're there you could apologize for being so offhand with him."

She stood up, went out to the kitchen, came back and thrust a cup of sugar into my hands.

"You borrowed it. You take it back."

I shook my head despairingly. "I told you – you're supposed to go. That's the rule. And when you get up there he's with this really pretty girl, and you think it's his girlfriend, but she turns out to be his sister and—"

"What are you talking about?"

"Then you all have a jolly good laugh about it and then you say you're having a little get-together and would he like to pop..."

"Terri! You're talking utter rubbish! Just go up there, give him back his sugar and come down again. Don't dare say a word about me!"

"Oh, all right," I said, taking the cup and crossing my fingers at the same time.

Up on the sixth floor I pressed my ear to Greg's door, just to make sure he wasn't At Home to another member of the acting profession. There was silence, but when I knocked I suddenly heard him intoning, *"To be, or not to be: That is the question"*, in a booming sort of way.

I tapped again and heard it again, and then he flung open the door holding the same script that he'd held the other evening.

He passed a hand across his brow. "Do excuse – just rehearsing my Hamlet," he said.

"Er ... do excuse, just returning the sugar," I said, handing over the cup.

He held it at arm's length. "*Is this a dagger I see before me?* No, it's a cup of sugar."

90

I laughed politely. "Sarah would have brought it back herself, but she's busy arranging this huge bunch of flowers that have just arrived from an admirer – some very rare orange pompon variety. Anyway, she said it was terribly kind of you to lend it to us."

"Anytime … anytime…" he said, making a dramatic gesture with the cup and scattering sugar everywhere.

"She said wasn't it amazing that you have such similar tastes in sugar and anytime you want to pop down to borrow anything from her you'd be very welcome."

"Did she really? How kind!" he said.

"Anytime…" I repeated. Preferably within the next three days, I thought.

"But, I did wonder … I mean, I didn't think your sister was all that pleased to see me before."

"Oh, no!" I said. "Quite the contrary." I lowered my voice. "You see, when Sarah meets someone she admires, she gets a bit tongue-tied. You know how it is – think how you'd be if you were suddenly to come face to face with someone you'd always fancied from afar."

His face furrowed so that he really did look a bit badger-like. "Yes. I see. I hadn't thought of it like that. I suppose sometimes the public *are* in awe of me."

"Exactly," I said. "But do come down anytime…"

When I got back to our flat the origami thing had been moved back to the top of the kitchen waste bin and Sarah and Loretta were deep in conversation on the settee. They eyed me, shook their heads and tutted.

Sarah said, "Now listen, you. Loretta's having a little supper for Brett tomorrow night."

"Yes," I said. "So what?"

"An intimate sort of supper."

I suddenly realized what they meant. "What, one with candles and wine and everything, to make him propose?"

Loretta rolled her eyes. "Absolute nightmare," she breathed. "One hint of that and he'll run a mile."

"Of course not to make him propose," Sarah said quickly. "Just a nice, quiet supper for two to thank him for the lots of times he's taken her out."

"What we're getting round to saying," Loretta went on, "is that you've got to stay out of the way. In your room. All evening. No coming out."

"Suppose I want to go to the loo?" I said. "Suppose I start coughing and want a drink of water? Suppose the house catches fire and..."

They both groaned.

"All right, all right, don't go on," said Sarah.

"You've got to think of these things," I said earnestly.

"We mean," Sarah said, "that *on the whole* you've got to stay in your room. Naturally, you may come out for any emergencies."

I pulled a face. "Seems to me that I'm not wanted," I said, and flounced off.

"Whatever gave you that idea?" I heard Loretta say.

I flounced myself onto my bed. Intimate supper for two, huh? Who was she kidding? Loretta had obviously arranged this set-up to get him to propose to her – and it was up to me, for the sake of my sister's happiness, to make jolly sure he didn't.

8

FRIDAY

"Well, where are you going?" I said to Sarah the following evening while Loretta bustled about setting tables and putting out candlesticks. "Can't I come with you?"

"I'm going to the cinema with someone from work," she said, "and no, you can't come. I've still got my suspicions about you being at the bottom of all that fuss in the wine bar on Wednesday."

I rolled my eyes. "Just because someone was having a row about some old note they thought someone had…"

"Note? What note?" she interrupted sharply. "Who said anything about a note?"

Oops! I opened my eyes all wide and innocent. "No one. I mean, I just thought that's what it was. Because I know a lot about these sorts of things. I…"

"Look," she said, forgetting for the moment about the wine bar, "if you know all about these things, you'll know perfectly well that you're not wanted here tonight; you'll know that sometimes couples like to be alone together."

I looked at her, marvelling. "You're so brave," I said. "So brave and noble – sacrificing the great love of your life to your friend…"

"For God's sake!" Her eyes gleamed angrily – or maybe they were flashing with pain and jealousy. "Just stay in your room, OK? Just stay in your room and you can't go wrong."

"All right, I'll stay locked away," I said, and then I added quietly, so she couldn't hear, "most of the time."

An hour later, I ventured to poke my head round my bedroom door. "Do you think I could possibly come out, Loretta?" I asked in a timid voice. I'd heard the tape deck go on (smoochy music), I'd heard Loretta fiddling around in the kitchen, and then I'd heard the bell go and Brett arrive. After that had come a bit of silence when I presumed they were having a snog. They'd had four and a half minutes on their own before I spoke up.

Loretta was standing by the table pouring Brett a drink, and she turned to me looking dead irritable but trying not to show it. I bristled a bit when I saw that look. I mean, it's all very well having your sister irritated with you and bossing you about – that's normal, really – but to have *her* do it wasn't on. She hadn't ever been nice to me, she didn't act at all like the *Girls Upstairs* girls did when their sisters came visiting.

"Of course you can come out," she said. "There's not a padlock on your door, is there?"

"Only you said to keep out of the way, and I didn't want to Interrupt Anything," I said, tiptoeing with exaggerated care towards the kitchen. "I just wanted to get myself a drink of water."

"You won't be interrupting anything," she said grittily. "Go right ahead."

"Don't you want to come out and watch TV?" Brett asked. He was sitting on the settee wearing a navy silk shirt and tight white jeans. He looked dead handsome – like the lead singer in a band.

"Ooh, no." I cast a nervous look at Loretta's back. "As I said, I wouldn't want to Interrupt Anything." I dropped my voice. "Loretta 'specially said I was to keep out of the way, you see. Stay in my room and not budge unless there was a fire. I'm allowed out if the house is burning down."

"I didn't exactly say that, Terri," Loretta said, smiling tightly. "I just thought it would be nice for Brett and me to have a quiet meal on our own." Pause. "Seems as if that's not possible, though," she added to herself.

I didn't say anything, just smiled and went towards the kitchen humming the wedding march under my breath. I knew from what Sarah had said that Brett was scared of being hooked – so all I had to do was make him think that Loretta was desperate to marry him!

Out of the corner of my eye I saw him suddenly realize what I was humming and go all frozen round his manly jaw.

Loretta followed me into the kitchen and poked me in the ribs. "Do you have to hum that?"

"Hum what?" I asked in a loud stage whisper.

"The wedding march!" She pursed her lips, sprinkled parsley on something, put something under the grill, poured cream over something else.

"Oops! Was that what it was? I didn't realize." I clapped my hand to my mouth. "Oh no, you don't want him to think you've invited him here to get him to propose, do you?"

Loretta glowered at me. "You're quite pathetic," she said in an acutely withering voice.

Well, I might have felt squashed, but instead I felt a wave of crusading spirit. "Do you think it's true that the way to a man's heart is through his stomach?" I enquired loudly of her. She didn't reply so I went on. "It's worth a try, I suppose. They like home cooking, don't they?"

Then I said, "Shall I take all these tins and foil containers downstairs to the dustbin for you?"

"Bed!" she commanded, as if my name was Rover, and pointed towards the door.

I stood my ground in the kitchen and drank my water, considering my next move. My sister's future was at stake here. OK, when it came to it she might not choose Brett, she might go for Greg or Simon instead, but at least she should have the choice. And anyway, it was out-and-out war between me and Loretta now.

Brett had turned on the TV by the time I wandered back in to the sitting room and was sitting with his nose about two inches from the screen, watching a fashion show featuring skimpy beach-wear.

"Look at that! Bit of all right, eh? Wouldn't mind seeing that in Lanzarote next summer!"

"Sarah's got a bikini like that," I nodded towards the screen, "and she looks much better in it." I squashed myself between the TV and him. "She's gone out to see a film," I said slowly and thoughtfully.

"Uh-huh." He tried to peer round me.

"She's been acting so strangely lately," I sighed. "Acting sort of bitter and heartbroken, if you know what I mean."

"No, I don't." By throwing himself to the other end of the settee he managed to see the screen, but they were wearing evening-wear now and he lost interest.

"I'm not sure exactly what it is, but she seems to be regretting something. Keeps sighing and looking out of the window whenever you…" I gasped suddenly, bit my lip. "Oh, I hope I haven't said too much!"

He gawped at me. "What d'you mean?"

I tried to keep my wistful look going while I waited for him to catch on. Just as I was thinking that I'd have to spell it out, Loretta came through from the kitchen.

"Starters!" she trilled, placing two small plates on the table. "Good night, Terri."

I jumped up. "Shall I change the tape?" I asked helpfully. "I'll see if we've got some special music to propo—" I stopped dead as Loretta's look almost bit me in half. "Shall I light the candles? They make a place look so romantic, don't they?"

"Absolute nightmare," Loretta muttered. "I can manage the candles, and I'm sure you've got things to do in your room, Terri."

"Not really," I said. I hung over the table, looking at what she was giving him: a square brown lump with some cold toast next to it. "That looks interesting. What is it?"

"Pâté," Loretta said grimly.

"Patty! That's a funny name, isn't it? Looks a bit funny, too. Like cat food. Not that I really know what cat food looks like because we haven't got a cat. We've got a gerbil. But it went up the chimney."

"Fascinating," Loretta said. "Don't let us keep you."

I peered closely at the plates. "What does it taste like? Can I have a bit of a lick, to try?"

"Terri…" said Loretta in a narrow, warning voice.

Brett was grinning, so I thought it was worth hanging on a moment or two longer. "Sorry! I was just being entertaining," I said brightly. "Mum likes me to be entertaining when we've got visitors. Terri, go and be entertaining, she says, and I…"

Loretta gave a short scream.

"OK, OK, I'm going!" And I was – but then the phone rang.

"Perhaps you'd get that on your way to your room," Loretta said.

It was Simon.

"I was just ringing to see if Sarah liked the flowers," he said with a token sniff.

I closed my eyes to a mental picture of them at the bottom of the bin. "Loved them," I said, turning aside so those at the table couldn't hear me. "Although a slightly bigger bunch wouldn't go amiss next time, Simon."

"I suppose Sarah's not there?" he asked.

"Afraid not."

"It's just as well… I feel rather queasy. Slight travel sickness from the bus home. And my head cold isn't getting any better, either."

"Oh, dear," I said briskly – even I was

getting bored with his symptoms. "I'll tell Sarah you rang, shall I?"

He sneezed. "If you would. And *do* you think I ought to get her another bunch of flowers?"

I smiled at the receiver. How gratifying that some people wanted my advice.

"Or should I try something else?" he went on. "Sweets or ... or a nice Swiss roll, perhaps?"

"Not a Swiss roll," I said hastily. "They're not exactly romantic, are they? Perhaps..." There flashed before me an instant replay of an old film I'd seen on TV where a man had sent his Beloved a beautiful basket of exotic fruit all covered in rustling cellophane and topped by a huge pink bow. "Fruit!" I said excitedly. "She likes fruit." I liked it, as well.

"Fruit?"

"Fruit will definitely do the trick," I said. "This could be your big chance, Simon!"

"Yes. All right." I heard one last sniff before he put down the phone.

"I don't know! Another one of Sarah's admirers!" I called towards Loretta and Brett, but they both ignored me.

Back in my room, I put Simon on the *Messages from Men* list, then got out a fresh piece of paper and, as Jo in *Girls Upstairs* had done only the week before, reviewed the options. In *Girls Upstairs* they always do a chart when they're unsure about which man to choose, and what happens then is that the man who comes out least likely, the one who gets the fewest points, is always the one they end up with. I could never make this out, but when I'd asked Mum why it was, she'd said it was to stand everything on its head and surprise the reader.

I made up my chart with three headings: SIMON; BRETT; GREG.

For SIMON I put: *Needs to be a bit more manly. Seems to be ill a lot. Could possibly be made into something with lots of help and encouragement. Rating with S: She doesn't seem keen. If she likes him but is playing hard to get she's overdoing the hard bit. Overall points out of ten: 4.*

BRETT: *Needs to be a bit less manly. Don't like the way he ogles girls on TV. L is throwing herself at him but he must be made to see that S is the better catch – that's if it's not too late after tonight. Rating with S: Probably very high but she is careful to keep her unbridled passion bridled. Overall points out of ten: 6.*

GREG: *Little bit showy, but then he's an actor so this is to be expected. Friendly and bouncy. Would be good to boast about at school, also he could get me into TV shows. Rating with S: dodgy at moment, but when she sees his potential – film premières and award ceremonies – she'll be hooked. Overall points out of ten: 8.*

NOTE: *In further dealings with all men, remember the key word:* subtle.

I surveyed the sheet. That meant, according

to the *Girls Upstairs* system, that Sarah was going to end up with Simon.

I stared for some time, thinking about having drippy Simon – half man, half lettuce – in the family, and wondering what I could do about it. Then I realized – if I altered the ratings, giving Simon the highest score and Greg the lowest, she'd end up with Greg instead!

I swopped their two scores and wrote at the bottom of the page: *Simon has the highest score, therefore Sarah will end up with him* – just to surprise myself even more when the time came.

As the evening went on I came out of my room four more times, either for drinks or to go to the loo.

"Sorry," I said on the final occasion. "Can't think why I keep needing to go."

"Could it be all the pints of water you've been drinking?" Loretta asked sarcastically, following me into the kitchen for another bottle of wine.

"Has he proposed yet?"

She gave me an evil look. "Mind your own business."

"Just asking!" I needed to know the state of play with the middle one on the chart. Jaz, Jan and Jo had never gone for the middle option, but there was always a first time for everything.

And meanwhile it was surely Greg's turn for a spot of encouragement. Luckily my sister was taking the next day off...

9

SATURDAY

"So what do you think?" I said to Mrs B. "Should I pretend he's ill or something and get her to go up there to give him the kiss of life, or should I push something of hers under the door of his flat and then tell her I put it there by mistake?"

"The thing you need," Mrs B said, tucking a red silk rose behind one ear, "is a social gathering. You've got to hold a coffee morning in your flat and invite him and everyone else in the house, so they can all get to know each other."

"If I do that, though," I said, "he might meet one of the girls from the other flats and fancy her and not Sarah."

"Mmm, that's a point," said Mrs B. "Even if they are all couples – that's never stopped anyone before." She drummed her fingers on a book called, *Trapped in Toronto!* "No," she went on after a moment, "you've got to be crafty. You tell Mr Golightly that it's a proper social gathering for everyone in the house, so that he doesn't feel he's being set up, but you don't actually invite anyone but him. That way your sister gets him all to herself."

"And what shall I tell her?"

Mrs B shrugged. "Wait until he appears and then just say he's come down for coffee. Nothing more natural than that."

"I think she might suspect…"

"Course she will, but you're going home on Monday, aren't you? You haven't got time for the niceties now, ducks. You've just got to get things moving."

"We're having a social gathering," I told Greg when he opened his door to me. "In our flat. This morning. Everyone for coffee! My sister asked me to come up and invite you specially."

He put his head on one side and beamed. He was wearing red boots and yellow dungarees and looked exactly like a children's TV presenter. "Sounds good to me!"

"We often have these social gatherings," I said chattily. "Everyone in the house comes. They just turn up, you know, *al fresco* and all that, and meet and greet each other."

"Sounds fun, fun, fun!"

"So will you come?" He did a little frisky sidestep. "Mr Brock, be he ever so busy, wouldn't pass up an opportunity like this!"

I looked at my watch. "In about fifteen minutes?" That would give me enough time to get Sarah cleaned up. "You do know which one my sister is, don't you? The one with long fair hair – not the pointy-nose who doesn't do a stroke of work around the house."

"I know her!" He made a flourishy gesture with his hand. "Hers is the face that launched a thousand ships!"

"Er ... yes," I said, going down the stairs. "See you soon, then."

Back in the flat, Loretta was sprawled reading the paper and Sarah was dashing about wearing a grey matted sweatshirt and old jeans.

I looked her up and down. "Wouldn't you like to wear something else today?" I asked.

"What for?"

"Just in case..."

"In case what?"

I shrugged carelessly. "In case someone comes for coffee or something."

She narrowed her eyes at me suspiciously, but before she could say anything there was a tap at the door. I jumped, but it was just a man wanting to read the electricity meter. Loretta let him in and took him to the cupboard where the meter was.

Sarah collected an armful of mugs and took them through to the kitchen to wash up. "I'm not wearing anything good," she said, "because

I'm going to the hairdresser's in a minute. I've got Señor Anton and he's a bit messy – I usually end up with mousse and bits of hair all over me."

I looked at her, startled. She hadn't told me she was going out! For a moment I toyed with the idea of adding Señor Anton to the Possibles list – but decided I couldn't take on anyone new at this late stage. No, what I had to do was keep her here...

I bit my lip and tried to look wistful. "Oh, do you *have* to go out?"

"Of course I do," she said. "Getting a Saturday appointment is murder; I had to book it five weeks ago. Come with me if you want. You'll be bored to tears but..."

"No, I don't want to come with you," I said. "I just ... just want you to stay here so we can have a nice talk."

She ran a sinkful of water and began wiping worktops. "Don't be silly. You can talk to me at the hairdresser's just as well."

"Because I'm feeling a bit homesick," I went on sadly, "missing Mum and wondering if the gerbil has come down the chimney."

"You're seeing Mum the day after tomorrow. How come you haven't said anything about missing her before? And you've never even mentioned the gerbil!"

Before I could elaborate on my heart-rending tale, the phone rang.

"Get that, will you?" said Sarah. "I'm running late."

It was Brett wanting Loretta – who was still with the meter man, holding his torch for him.

"She's not available at the moment," I said. "She's ... with someone."

"What sort of someone?"

"A man," I said. "In uniform."

There was a moment's silence while he digested this. "What are they doing?"

"I can't quite see," I said. "They're in a small cupboard together."

"Yeah?" he said indignantly. "You don't say." Another pause. "Er ... about your sister being heartbroken."

"Yes?" I had to be careful – at that moment Sarah (putting on shoes and mascara at the same time) was rushing past.

"You *did* say heartbroken?"

"Completely. Though it's difficult to go into it at the moment, if you see what I mean."

"Right!" he said. "I'll call round and see her some time, shall I? Have a quiet chat with her about it."

"Good idea," I said, trying to sound normal. It had worked! I'd got him thinking Sarah was still madly in love with him. "I think you should do that as soon as possible."

"And ask Loretta to ring me, will you, er ... Thingy."

"Will do," I said.

"Who was that?" Sarah asked when I replaced the receiver.

"Brett," I said, pouncing on her make-up bag, grabbing her lipstick and hiding it up my sleeve. "He wants Loretta to ring him."

"All that time just to say that?" She started looking for her lipstick. "He's usually a man of few words."

"They do say that a man of few words has much to hide." I'd read that in a magazine only the day before.

"My lipstick! Where's it gone?" she screeched. She emptied her make-up bag, then pulled all the cushions off the settee. "I look half dead without it."

I pushed the Brett development to one side and concentrated on Greg. It was vital I boosted his standing before he arrived. "I think Greg upstairs is very nice," I said.

"I had it here a moment ago..."

"And he really likes you. He said your face ... er ... launched a boat."

She pulled out six ballpoint pens and a lot of fluff from the back of the settee. "What? What on earth are you talking about?"

"He said something about boats, anyway. Or ships."

"I expect he was rehearsing an advert for ships' rivets," she said. "That's about all he's good for."

I was shocked. "Don't be like that! He's a proper actor. When I saw him the other day he was doing *Hamlet*..."

There was another tap at the door and I sprang to open it. Greg was standing there, still in the dungarees and now with a matching baseball cap set at an angle.

"Greg Golightly at your service!" he cried. "Golightly by name, Golightly by..." He looked round for his audience, saw only me, and trailed off.

"That's nice! You're first!" I said, and I led him through to where Sarah was on all fours looking under an armchair. She turned and stared at him. She had a sort of What-on-earth's-he-want? look on her face, but I didn't give her a chance to actually say it.

"Greg has come for coffee!" I said. "Isn't that nice!"

She straightened up. "It's rather inconvenient, actually. I'm already ten minutes late for my hairdresser's appointment. Perhaps Loretta would like to do the honours, Terri."

For a moment I was stumped. The last thing I wanted was for *her* to snaffle him. But Greg came up trumps.

"If you're late for an appointment and as it has just started to rain," he said, "might I offer you a lift in my car?"

"No, really..."

"What a brilliant idea!" I said. With a cry of

110

surprise, I found the lipstick and threw it to Sarah.

"But…"

"If you miss this Saturday you'll probably have to wait till Christmas!"

"It'll be no trouble, I assure you!" said Greg. "My little orange Beetle awaits!"

"Señor Anton might never speak to you again!"

"Well…"

She was torn, I knew it. I was nearly there! I picked up her handbag and made sure her keys were in it, got her jacket off the hook behind the door.

"The buses *can* be dodgy on a Saturday…" she said.

I fiddled her arm into one jacket sleeve, flung the rest of the jacket over her shoulder and hung her bag over the top. I propelled her towards the door.

"Bye, Loretta!" I shouted as we went out, wondering if she was still in the cupboard with the meter man.

Going down the stairs, I was desperate for Mrs B to appear and witness my success, but we reached street level without seeing anyone at all. Never mind, I thought, this is brilliant. He's bound to offer to collect her afterwards, and then – well, who knew what might happen? He might just drive off with her into the sunset.

For at least two minutes I thought I had it made. Then, just as Greg was unlocking the car door, disaster struck.

There was a sneeze behind us and we turned to see Simon standing there holding half of a very large water melon and looking cross. I recognized the melon – it was the one that had been sitting outside the corner shop all week with a *Reduced for Quick Sale* sticker on it.

We all stared.

"Fruit!" Simon spluttered indignantly. "You said to buy fruit. You said it would do the trick. Well, I buy fruit and what do I find? She's going out with someone else!"

"Ooh ... er..." I began, wondering if it was the right time to mention my vision of the cellophane-wrapped basket with the pink bow on top.

"Well, you can have your fruit!" Simon said, and he shoved the melon at Sarah and Greg, turned tail and strode off. In quite a manly way, actually.

There was an exclamation of horror from Greg, who got the worst of it. The melon was overripe, soft and soggy. It split on impact, leaving Sarah with soft squashy bits down her jeans and Greg decorated with seeds. They slithered down the front of his dungarees and dropped gently onto his red suede boots.

Outraged shrieks: Sarah turned on me. "You little—"

"I didn't know, did I?" I said, backing away. "How could I have known he was going to do that? I thought he was buying fruit done up in a basket with a pink bow on top!"

Greg stood there looking as if a lot of the bounce had gone out of him.

"I'll just go and get something to clean you both up, shall I?" I said as I retreated indoors.

As I ran across the hall, Mrs B popped out. "How's it going, ducks?" she said.

"Not all that well, actually." We heard the roar of Greg's Beetle outside. I told Mrs B what had happened.

"Sarah will end up killing me," I finished. "And then Greg and Simon will probably kill me as well."

"No, no, that'll be all right," Mrs B said. "It's just what they need."

I looked out of the window – Sarah wasn't there. Had she actually gone with Greg?

"How d'you work that out?" I asked.

"Well," Mrs B said, "stands to reason. Mr Golightly will see that someone else likes her, so he'll be all the keener. And so will Simon. They'll both be trying twice as hard from now on!"

"Is that what you think?" I asked, brightening slightly.

"Course I do. You go and pick all that mess off my pavement and then come in and have a nice cup of black coffee."

10

SUNDAY

"I'm not allowed outside the front door," I said mournfully to Mrs B next morning. I'd gone to her for sympathy before Sarah and Loretta were up. "I'm not allowed out, not allowed to answer the phone – not even allowed to look out of the window!"

"You don't say," said Mrs B, tutting.

"They're both going off for lunch and they say I've just got to sit quietly in the flat all day and think about what I've done."

"Dear, oh dear…"

"I mean, I was only trying, wasn't I? Just doing my best. I said to her: Sarah, I did what I did for the sake of your happiness. I was trying to help you."

"And what did she say?"

"She didn't say anything – not to me. She won't speak to me. 'Keep her away from me,

Loretta,' she said. 'Just keep her out of my sight or I might do something I won't regret.' And of course, Loretta is only too pleased to have extra reasons to be nasty to me."

"Coffee, dear?" Mrs B asked. I nodded glumly. She wove her way through the furniture to the kitchen and I heard the kettle go on. "So, let me get this straight," she said from the doorway. "After the melon incident, your sister *didn't* go off with Mr Golightly?"

"No! She was telling someone on the phone last night: a bus came along and she was so embarrassed, she just jumped on."

"Oh, my!"

"And I had to promise, practically swear in blood, that I wouldn't do anything else – that I wouldn't even *speak* to another man until I got home. And then they found my Possibles list and tore it up in front of me."

Mrs B came back with two mugs of coffee. When she passed mine over, I was pleased to see she'd forgotten I liked it black.

"My last day in London and I'm going to be stuck inside, all by myself," I said dourly. "I tell you, the next time I come here I'm not even going to *try* to be helpful. I'm just going to watch her being bitter and twisted and let her get on with it. She can envy Elizabeth till she's blue in the face, I'm not going to do anything about it."

"That will jolly well serve her right!"

"There's just one thing that's worrying me…"

"What's that, ducks?"

"Brett – the one Loretta's got her claws into. He told me he'd come and see Sarah, and if he comes round while I'm still here – " I blew out my cheeks and made an explosive sound, "Sarah's going to go mad. She'll chop me into little pieces."

Mrs B patted my hand reassuringly. "Let's just hope he doesn't come until after you've gone, then."

Both Sarah and Loretta were up when I got back. They were in the kitchen talking in low voices.

"He's just acting strangely," I heard Loretta say. "As if he's not really with me, you know. As if he's preoccupied with something – or somebody – else."

"Are you seeing him today?" Sarah asked.

"No. I promised to go to the cinema with Avril."

"Could he be having trouble at work?"

"I don't think so." Loretta's voice went hard. "I'm sure he's going out with somebody else – either that or he'd like to. The rot set in that night he came round here for supper and heard your blasted sister humming the wedding march."

"Little beast!" Sarah said. "I don't know how I got talked into having her here, I really don't.

When I think what trouble she's caused…"
She opened the kitchen door suddenly and
discovered me standing there.

"Eavesdroppers never hear good of themselves," she said coldly. "And how true that is
in your case."

I gave her my sunniest smile. At least she
was talking to me again.

That afternoon, when they'd both gone out,
I stalked round the flat looking for something
to do. There was nothing on TV, I'd read my
mags millions of times, and I had nothing
to look forward to except going home and
organizing a gerbil search party. It wasn't even
as if I'd be able to go back to school amidst
congratulations on having brought True Love
into my sister's life. No, True Love, as far as I
could see, existed only in stories.

But as I thought about Jaz, Jan and Jo and
all their romantic ups and downs, I knew that
I still believed in it all. I'd told Mrs B that I'd
never do anything to help Sarah ever again –
but I hadn't really meant it. In spite of everything, I couldn't squash the faint hope that
something I'd kindled during my stay might
still burst into flame.

Maybe Simon had had the shock he needed
– maybe he'd turn more manly overnight and
his sniff would disappear. Maybe Brett (after
I'd gone safely home, please) would come
round and he and Sarah would Suddenly

Realize. Maybe Greg would stop singing the Mr Brock song, and reveal his serious, Hamlet side.

No, I wasn't going to give up. On the surface I was, but not underneath. I felt cheered. I looked round again for something to do, found the melon seeds in the bin, a skewer and some string, and started threading the seeds into bracelets.

I was wondering whether I could sell them at school, and feeling much better, when the bell rang. I went to answer it, conveniently forgetting I wasn't allowed to.

To my surprise – and in my head I immediately recreated the Possibles list – there stood Simon with a carton of wine gums.

He thrust them at me. "Give these to Sarah to say I'm sorry, will you?" He blew his nose lavishly. "I must have had a funny turn yesterday; don't know what came over me." He brightened. "Maybe it was some new virus or other."

I examined the carton for *reduced* stickers. "What – a throwing-melons-at-people virus?"

"Something like that," he said. He thrust the handkerchief back into a bulging jacket pocket. "I suppose I couldn't give the sweets to her myself?"

"She's not in at the moment," I said.

"I could wait…"

I thought quickly. How could I help it that

he had called? I'd just been sitting quietly making melon-seed bracelets – it was absolutely nothing to do with me if someone turned up bearing wine gums.

"She won't be long," I said, opening the door wider to let him in. "She's gone for lunch with a friend from work. You can sit and help me string melon seeds if you like."

We went upstairs, I settled him with a pile of seeds and he was getting on with them quite nicely when there was a sharp rap on our door and there stood Greg.

"Came to present a bill to someone for my red suede boots," he said. He caught sight of Simon bent over his colander. "You'll do!"

He bounced through and Simon, somewhat alarmed, stood up quickly, dropping the colander on the floor. "I really didn't mean … just felt a trifle light-headed yesterday. Most out of character, really…"

"That's as may be," Greg said, "but I've got an audition on Tuesday for tomato purée. I was planning on being in scarlet from head to toe. The whole concept's ruined."

He thrust his bill at Simon, who looked at it and – well, he was pale and doleful-looking anyway, but he went even paler. "I really don't think…" he began, and frowned at the box of wine gums as if to say he'd already had considerable expense that day.

"Well, someone's going to pay for them!"

said Greg, and he turned to me quite fiercely for someone who'd made his name as cuddly Mr Brock.

"Perhaps you'd better wait and see Sarah, too," I suggested.

Visions of pistols at dawn swam into my mind, and my spirits soared. No one in my magazines had ever had a *duel*!

Greg and Simon sat down – but there was hardly a moment to savour the romantic possibility of a dawn meeting on a hillside, with Sarah (wearing a black cloak) wringing her hands in the background, when the bell went again.

All the way down those stairs I knew with dreadful certainty who it must be. I only hoped I'd be wrong.

I wasn't.

Brett was wearing a white T-shirt and had a black leather jacket slung over his shoulders.

"Loretta's out today, isn't she?" he asked. "Thought I'd pop over while the coast was clear and ... you know ... sort out your sister's problem."

"Sarah's not in at the moment," I said faintly.

"That's OK. I'll wait!" he said, and as I closed the front door he was already running up the stairs two at a time.

I followed more slowly. Well, it wasn't my fault they'd all turned up like this, was it?

How could I help it?

By the time I'd reached the flat I'd decided there was nothing else for it: I'd line them up ready and Sarah would just have to choose when she got home. In the meantime they could sit quietly and help me make melon-seed bracelets.

Sarah arrived about ten minutes later, and by then I was having trouble keeping the three of them in order. No one except Simon would even *look* at the melon seeds.

"Terri! I'm back!" she called, "and I've brought someone with me, to meet you."

"I've … er … got someone here to meet you, as well," I said, suddenly nervous. "Three someones!"

She came to the kitchen door, and behind her was a tall man with dark hair. He had a tweedy jacket and looked about thirty.

"This is Peter from work," she said, "my boss and also…" she came fully into the room, saw the assembled company and stopped dead.

"This is … er … Brett and Greg and Simon," I said brightly.

"Terri!" Sarah shrieked.

"They came to … er … help me make melon-seed bracelets."

The three suitors looked at her, then at the man she was with, and for a moment no one moved. It was Simon who broke the spell – he suddenly thrust his box of wine gums at her. Then Greg snatched the cleaning bill from Simon and thrust *that* at her. Brett said distantly, "Tell Loretta I called, will you?" and they all disappeared.

Sarah backed out of the kitchen and sat down heavily on the arm of a chair, clutching the wine gums and the bill. "Tell me I'm dreaming," she said. "Tell me I didn't come in just now and see those three standing there waiting for me."

"I didn't ask them to come round!" I began. "I didn't say anything. They just arrived and I couldn't get rid of them!"

The Peter man sat in the armchair and began laughing. "I've been wondering about you, Sarah, and now I know! You've got a secret stock of men and when I'm not around you go to the cupboard and take one out!"

I stared at him. I hadn't taken in what he'd said because I was looking at the way he was *ruffling Sarah's hair*.

Then she started laughing, too. She threw the wine gums up in the air. "Such an extravagant, devoted lot!" Now I was staring at her because *her head was on his shoulder*.

"It's a good job we came home when we did, otherwise I would never have found out," he said, *pulling her into his lap*.

Sarah shook her head at me. "I don't know what you've been doing here, Terri. All I can say is thank God you're going home tomorrow!"

"Well, you see, it's just that I thought you were all bitter and twisted..." I began, forgetting for the moment the perfect scene from *Girls Upstairs* being played out in front of my eyes and concentrating on getting out of trouble. "And when you said about wanting to get married like Elizabeth I thought..."

"I've never said that!"

"You did! I heard you. You and Loretta were talking and you said how lucky Elizabeth was and if only that could be you..."

"I meant how lucky to get a job like hers – she's going to travel all over the world!" Sarah said. She glanced at Peter. "Liz is a computer scientist, you know – she was head-hunted by an American firm."

"You told me she left here to get married!" I said.

"Oh, that as well. But mostly because of her new job."

I frowned deeply, trying to come to terms with this. "So you didn't ... you're not..." I struggled, very distracted by the fact that he was kissing her nose.

Sarah kissed him back and then she looked at me and said, "It might have been easier if I'd told you earlier. It might have saved all the aggro."

"Told me what?"

"About Peter," she said. "I mean, I thought I'd dropped enough hints – about going out with 'a friend from work' and how nice the managers were. I thought you might have realized that I had someone."

"We're an item," Peter said. "I think that's what they call it."

"Why didn't you tell me as soon as I got here?" I burst out. To think I'd gone to all that trouble and she had someone all along!

"Well, for a start it's all very hush-hush," Sarah said. "We don't want anyone at work to know. And the other thing is, knowing what you're like – well, I knew, if I'd said about Peter, what the next question would be." She went a bit pink. "And as we haven't actually decided on anything like ... about ... that..."

"I think," Peter interrupted, "that we'd better sort things out right away – hurry up and get married in case you're forced to take up with one of the wine gum brigade. They looked pretty dodgy to me."

"Peter!" Sarah laughed.

I put up my hand. "Hang on a minute," I said, "and excuse my curiosity, but was that a proposal of marriage?"

"Probably," Sarah murmured, looking at him all soppily.

"And was it a proposal of marriage brought on by finding that there were three men waiting here in the flat when you came in?"

I asked excitedly.

They didn't reply, because they were kissing. But I knew that it was, and I knew that I'd caused the whole thing. Me. Entirely unaided.

Smiling, gloating, flapping my little cupid's wings behind me, I went downstairs to tell Mrs B it had all worked out and that True Love wasn't dead. Also to ask what colour she thought might suit me for a bridesmaid's dress.

BEST FRIENDS, WORST LUCK

Mary Hooper

"It's awful here. Boring. The village consists of about one house and half a shop... Adele hates it as well. We have to talk to each other because there's no one else."

When style-conscious, streetwise Bev moves from London to the Somerset farm of her new stepfather, she takes a packing-case full of prejudices with her. In her opinion, the country is a hell of mud, cows and hideously unfashionable yokels. Who will she and her older sister Adele find to talk to? How on earth will Bev manage without her best friend, Sal? And how will Sal manage without her? These are just a few of the crucial questions to be answered in this funny, lively and wonderfully perceptive story.

MORE WALKER PAPERBACKS
For You to Enjoy